A Tide of War

A Shade of Vampire, Book 41

Bella Forrest

Also by Bella Forrest:

An Hour of Need (Book 29)
A Game of Risk (Book 30)
A Twist of Fates (Book 31)
A Day of Glory (Book 32)

Series 5:
A Dawn of Guardians

A Dawn of Guardians (Book 33)
A Sword of Chance (Book 34)
A Race of Trials (Book 35)
A King of Shadow (Book 36)
An Empire of Stones (Book 37)
A Power of Old (Book 38)
A Rip of Realms (Book 39)

A SHADE OF DRAGON
TRILOGY :

A Shade of Dragon 1
A Shade of Dragon 2
A Shade of Dragon 3

A SHADE OF KIEV
TRILOGY:

A Shade of Kiev 1
A Shade of Kiev 2
A Shade of Kiev 3

DETECTIVE ERIN BOND
(Adult mystery/thriller)

Lights, Camera, Gone
Write, Edit, Kill

BEAUTIFUL MONSTER
DUOLOGY:

Beautiful Monster 1
Beautiful Monster 2

For an updated list of Bella's books, please visit her website:
www.bellaforrest.net

Join Bella's VIP email list and she'll personally send you an email
reminder as soon as her next book is out! Visit here to sign up:
www.forrestbooks.com

Contents

THE "NEW GENERATION" NAMES LIST

- **Arwen:** (daughter of Corrine and Ibrahim - witch)
- **Benedict:** (son of Rose and Caleb - human)
- **Brock:** (son of Kiev and Mona – half warlock)
- **Grace:** (daughter of Ben and River – half fae and half human)
- **Hazel:** (daughter of Rose and Caleb – human)
- **Heath:** (son of Jeriad and Sylvia – half dragon and half human)
- **Julian:** (son of Ashley and Landis)
- **Ruby:** (daughter of Claudia and Yuri – human)
- **Victoria:** (daughter of Vivienne and Xavier – human)

BENEDICT

We walked away from our family and friends, leaving them to face the enemy while we searched for the jinn that GASP and Tejus still believed could be hiding somewhere in Nevertide. I couldn't speak for Julian, but walking away—along the main road that crossed the land, in the opposite direction from the cove—was one of the hardest things I'd ever done.

I didn't look back. I kept my eyes on the road ahead, the map that Tejus had drawn clutched in my hand. There would be a turn-off that we had to take to make our way up to the Dauoa Forest. Until then, we just had to keep going straight, moving as briskly as we could. On the main path we were exposed, but the further we walked, the less I felt like we were in danger.

Nevertide felt like a ghost land. Empty land which had once been farmed was now burnt, smoke still wafting up into the sky. Parts of the earth had fallen into the craters caused by the earthquake—huge pits where the ground had just slid into nothingness, caverns so deep that none of us, not even the Hawks, Ridan or jinn, could make out the bottom.

Yelena walked by my side, but we didn't speak. In the distance, we could all hear the sounds of the battle starting. I doubted that any of us had much to say. We were all lost in our own thoughts, no doubt wondering whether or not any of this would be successful—the battle or our mission. And if it wasn't, how long we would manage to stay alive.

I was glad that we'd taken Ridan, Horatio and Aisha with us now. I'd been skeptical at first because it kind of felt like they were babysitting us, but I'd had my fair share of experiences in the forests of Nevertide and I didn't really relish the idea of venturing inside them again without some magic on our side.

Along with the two jinn and Ridan, the half-Hawk boys Field, Fly and Sky had joined us. I didn't know them very well, even though Field was technically my half-cousin, or something like that, but the Hawk boys tended to keep to themselves. They were friendly, but they intimidated me a little. Maybe it was because they looked so cool. They were all tall, with toned muscles that made them look tough despite their long hair, and I had always been jealous of their wings. They protruded from their shoulder blades, each feather as black as night and so sharp at the tip that they looked like daggers.

Yeah. The Hawks were badass, and sometimes I wished I was one of them.

I glanced over at Julian. For a while now he had been intermittently looking up at the sky. I guessed he was checking to see if we were being followed by the shadow. I didn't bother doing the same—we would all feel it long before we saw it, that strange sense of dread and sickness that swirled in the stomach and made the hairs on the back of our necks prick up.

"I think we turn here," I said, seeing an old, dilapidated stone barn. I checked the map that Tejus had made. The barn had been marked as the turning point. Now we would go off road, traveling north till we reached the forests.

"We should fly ahead," Field replied, turning to his brothers before looking off in the distance.

"Agreed," said Ridan. "Let's all meet again at the foot of the forests."

The landscape was bare, but it dipped and rose at certain points. Some of the grassy hills were so high that we could only see the tips of the mountains from where we stood.

"I can't actually tell from this map how far it is to the forest," I mused, staring down at the piece of paper that Tejus had shoved in my hand. It had been drawn in a hurry by the sentry, and there were no proper landmarks detailed from here to our destination.

"Hopefully not far," Fly replied. His gray-blue eyes scanned the torn sky, and the boy shuddered. "We'll check the coast is clear, then come back and pick you up."

The Hawk boys, in perfect unison, jumped up, springing off the balls of their feet. In mid-air, their wings expanded and they shot up into the sky, then soared off in the direction of the mountains—Ridan joining them.

"Wow," Yelena breathed, "they're *so* cool."

I sighed. "Yeah, they are."

"Wouldn't you want to fly if you could?" she murmured.

"Yeah… We should keep moving anyway." I started to head off the path, kicking the dry stones with the toes of my boots.

Horatio and Aisha followed us, speaking in hushed tones that I couldn't hear properly, but every so often I heard them mention Riza, their baby girl. I imagined they were both missing her.

My backpack was starting to feel heavy, and I trudged along, wishing that I had thought to ask the Hawks to carry us.

"They're heading back," Aisha announced, stopping.

I could see the faint pinpricks of the Hawks in the distance. I dropped my bag down and sat on it, waiting for them to arrive.

In a matter of moments, they dropped down on the ground gracefully, knees bent and arms outstretched, before their wings folded back up and they stood upright.

"It's not far," Field informed us. "But the forest is massive. It could take us days, months even, to search it properly. Ridan's waiting at the forest entrance for us."

I was startled by his assessment. None of the sentries had told us that the forest was that big. It worried me. We just didn't have that kind of time. We'd have to hope that luck was on our side or we'd be in major trouble.

"Don't worry." Horatio smiled at me. "Once we're in the forest, Aisha and I can try to feel them out. It should be easier once we're in their vicinity. They might have put up barriers around where they're hiding."

"What if it's only one of them? Will you be able to find just one?" I asked.

Aisha and Horatio looked at one another.

"It would be harder," Aisha conceded, "but not impossible. But it's unlikely that it will be one jinni on their own. We are tribal creatures, and from what we've seen of the entity's power, it doesn't sound like just one jinni could accomplish locking him in the stones."

"Okay." I nodded, feeling reassured. "Let's get going then."

"Aisha, Horatio, are you okay to get there on your own?" Field asked. "There's a tree stump directly in front of us, about three miles ahead. Let's meet there?"

"We'll be behind you. We're slower when we don't know the land," the jinni replied.

Field faced me, arms outstretched.

"Ready, little man?" he asked.

"Ready," I muttered. I turned around so that he wouldn't be carrying me like a baby. Field wrapped his arms around my waist and held on tight. Fly did the same to Yelena, who looked *way* over-excited, and Sky picked up Julian.

A split-second later we were hurtling through the sky—the ground miles below, the trees, fences and the occasional wooden hut all looking like they were part of a kid's model toy. Traveling by Hawk wasn't as comfortable as using vultures like the sentries did, but I certainly felt safer.

We touched down on the dry earth, facing the forest. I straightened out my t-shirt that had ridden up on the ride. Yelena looked a little bit dazed, and Julian seemed happy to have his feet back on solid ground. Ridan approached us from a nearby tree.

"I've seen nothing so far, but I don't like the feeling of the place," he announced. "we need to be careful."

A moment later, Horatio and Aisha appeared a few feet from the stump Field had mentioned. We all gazed at the forest.

"I've got a bad feeling about this," Julian said, his voice barely audible.

"I know what you mean," I replied.

"Ash saw goblins in here, and the blind wolf things that he and King Memenion had battled." He pulled a face, his fingers resting on the sword tied to his waist.

"I think Queen Trina was the worst thing in there though," I replied, trying to make myself feel better.

"We can fly ahead here too," Sky suggested. "Check there's nothing lying in wait. The place seems so quiet though…"

"That's what worries me," I muttered.

"It's unnatural," Aisha agreed. "The whole of this place is too quiet—not just the forest." The jinni looked around, shaking her head in disapproval.

Yelena tugged on my sleeve.

"We should get moving," she hissed. "Whatever's in that forest can't be worse than the shadow."

She was right. I might not like the silence, and the way the trees seemed to be *looking* at us like they were alive, but it was better than the shadow. Anything was.

"Okay. Yeah." I nodded to Field and Ridan. "Fly on ahead. Let us know if you see anything."

They leapt up into the air again, and the rest of us entered the forest on foot.

"We'll stay with you," Horatio murmured as we thwacked thorn branches down with our feet. I was grateful that the jinn wouldn't go on ahead—I had the feeling that we were unwelcome here. Whatever creatures had made the Dauoa forest their home certainly weren't friendly.

I picked up a fallen branch, removing the leafy twigs at the top till it made a walking stick—and weapon. Yelena did the same.

We stuck together, none of us wanting to veer ahead or lag behind. Field dropped in alone, making me jump, but only to tell us that the coast was clear for the next mile or so. I thanked him, and he flew on again. I looked up, trying to see the Hawk boys. I could hear the faint rustle of their feathers as they flew around us, but the trees were too densely packed together for my human eyes to make them out.

We carried on.

About a mile into the forest I stopped. The others did the same. I could distinctly hear rustling noises in the undergrowth that weren't being made by any of us.

"Guys…" Julian unsheathed his sword, his eyes darting in the direction of the noise—but it was surrounding us, fast.

"Stand back," Horatio demanded. He and Aisha stood in front of us, their eyes fixed on the forest floor.

The rustling stopped suddenly, and I heard a child-like giggle coming from behind a large bush. A second later, a group of about fourteen goblins had surrounded us. Their black, beady little eyes observed us with malice. One of them grinned, showing rows of razor-sharp teeth.

"Oh, for goodness' sake." Aisha sighed, smiling at Horatio.

He sniggered just as the goblins tore toward us, their claws reaching out, their mouths open.

Then, without warning, the goblins vanished.

"Huh? Where did they go?" I stared at the two jinn. Then I felt a sharp pain on my ankle, like a mosquito bite. Looking down, I realized that the goblins were still attacking...they were just now about the same size as my thumb.

"Ow!" I yelled, shaking the creature off me.

"Aww," Yelena cooed, bending down to inspect the horde of angry little goblins. She straightened up pretty quickly, rubbing her finger.

"That's cool." I grinned at Aisha.

"Couldn't you make them disappear?" Julian grumbled, kicking at them with his boots. "It's like we've just stepped on a hornets' nest."

Ridan, Field, Fly and Sky shot down, landing a few feet away.

"What's the hold-up?" Field asked.

"We were ambushed by goblins!" I said.

"Where?" growled the Hawk.

"Here," I replied, kicking one of them in his direction that was trying to scramble up onto my boot.

"Oh." The Hawks laughed.

Yeah. It was all *hilarious* when you had magic powers or wings. Try being mortal. Goblins didn't seem so funny then.

"Let's get moving," I sighed, picking my walking stick back up. I hoped Aisha and Horatio could deal with the rest of the creatures in the forest so easily—I had a feeling that the goblins would be the least of our problems.

RUBY

I didn't know how long it had taken me to get to Ghouls' Ridge. The passing of time stopped being measured in minutes and hours, and was replaced by Ash's labored breaths—eternities taking place between each inhale and exhale, never knowing if each would be his last.

I was dimly aware that the dawn was starting to rise as I reached the imposing cliff-face. How I'd even got to my destination was a mystery, and one that I owed to the bull-horse more than my own navigation.

The creature came to a standstill right by the entrance to the small passage which would lead to the Impartial Ministers' home. It could go no further, and it would be up to me to carry Ash's body through the narrow opening where the cliff met the sides of the valley.

"Ash?" I whispered, moving the hair from his brow. His skin was cold and damp. He groaned, but his eyes were closed. Before I disembarked from the bull-horse, I checked his wound. The blood had slowed down to a trickle, but he'd lost a lot of it. The GASP-issue shirt I'd pressed against the open wound was soaked through. I hated the idea of moving him, terrified of making the wound worse, but I had no choice—the immortal waters might be the only way I could save him.

Clambering down from the animal, I tied the reins to a withered tree nearby that was growing out of the rocks. Next, I gently pulled Ash down from the bull-horse. I wouldn't be able to carry him, but I could lean him against me, half dragging him along, if he wasn't able to walk.

"Ash, this is going to hurt. I'm sorry."

I gritted my teeth, forcing my body to take his weight. His breathing quickened when I moved him, coming out in rasps. The blood from his wound increased, flowing freely as I shuffled us both along the passage. A line of dark crimson trailed along behind us.

"Not long now," I promised.

I moved us both into the light of the Impartial Ministers' strange domain. Where it had been dark outside, the sky in here was still bright blue. I wondered if it was ever night here, or if the sky even changed color at all.

It was easier to move Ash on the polished marble floor, and for a while the only sounds I could hear were the pain-filled grunts of Ash, my own huffs of effort, and the sound of Ash's boots staggering along the floor. I felt like I was going crazy. No matter how much effort I put into heaving us forward, the basin of water seemed to remain in the distance, just out of reach.

"Oh, just give me a *break*," I half-sobbed to the empty chamber. I was so desperate, so panicked. A hot flush was starting to run down my back, the kind of uncomfortable prickly heat that made me want to scream.

We finally made it over to the edge of the basin. The waters remained, still and silent, the dancing white light shimmering beneath the surface. Even though we'd taken gallons with us when the warlocks and witches came to infuse the weapons, the water level seemed completely unchanged, as if we'd never been here at all.

I left Ash lying at the edge of the pool, and I jumped in. The water was cool. Instantly the heat of my body died down, every aching muscle soothed, my racing heart slowing to a steady beat.

This is going to work.

I could feel it. I waded back over to Ash, pulling him in alongside me. I removed his robe, shoving it back over the side, and laid him on his back, submerging his entire body in the water except his mouth and eyes.

Within moments, the water blushed red with Ash's blood. My earlier certainty was suddenly replaced with doubt. If the water encouraged more blood to leave his body, would I have made matters worse?

"Ash! Ash, please wake up," I begged, shaking him as his body floated just below the surface. Not knowing what to do, I rested my head on his shoulder, the water now ice-cold and making my teeth rattle.

"Please. I'm begging you, Ash," I whispered hoarsely. "I don't know if you can hear me or not. But can you please just wake up— can you please just be okay—because I can't, I really *can't* do this without you. I know I'm selfish. I want you to live for me. I *need* you to do that, so I don't completely fall apart. I'm scared how I'll feel if you don't get through this…I'm scared of the pain, Ash. *Please.*"

I could feel his heartbeat, barely there, but just about discernible. Looking down at the wound I saw no change, the blood still curling off into the waters. I was about to move out—taking Ash back to my parents was probably my only other option now—but as I waded us both to the side of the basin, the pool shuddered beneath me.

For a moment, I thought it was another earthquake about to erupt, but the movement was only slight, and seemed to be coming from the depths of the pool. The waters started to ripple from the center outwards. I looked down at the light at the bottom. It was pulsing, as if it had its own heartbeat, growing brighter by the second.

I held onto Ash with a shaking hand.

The water started to change color. Ash's blood started to draw together, removing the red stain from the water and concentrating it in a whirlpool in the center. It started to move toward Ash. Where the water was lapping over his wound, the whirlpool broke, sending his blood to be diluted again, until it was drawn back into the center of the pool.

It's trying to heal him, I realized.

Taking a deep breath, I pushed Ash's body down, drowning him in the immortal waters.

Now the whirlpool could latch onto his wound. Staggering back, I watched in amazement as the stream of blood poured itself back into the wound, any taint of red leaving the water completely. His skin started to close itself, the violent gashes caused by the shadow becoming smaller and smaller.

I moved to raise him up from beneath the water, worried he couldn't breathe. The second my fingers touched him, a bright, brilliant light flared up from his body, blinding me. I fell back, shielding my face. Losing my balance, I dropped into the water. My eyes opened for the briefest moment, and I saw an eternity of white light. It didn't feel like I was in the pool anymore, but in a pure void of nothingness—almost the opposite of what the entity had created when it had ripped open the sky.

I pushed up to the surface, gasping for breath. I looked around wildly, reassured to see I was back in the pool, but Ash was still fully submerged in the water. I waded over to him as quickly as I could. The light had vanished completely, and Ash was just floating beneath the surface, eyes still closed, no bubbles coming from his nose or mouth.

"ASH!" I cried, dragging him up by his shoulders.

I held him upright in the water, clutching his body to mine, praying that he would wake up. I thumped him, hard, on the back.

He coughed, a stream of water falling from his mouth. A second later his eyes opened. His brown irises looked lighter than I'd ever seen them, but they were still the warm, almost gold, earthen hue that always made me think Ash was so solid and dependable.

"Ruby?" he whispered, his voice tentative.

His eyes came to rest on mine, the confusion vanishing. He hacked again, but this time he squeezed my shoulders as he did so.

"Hey, you." I smiled. I was fighting back tears, and the effort of doing so made my chest heave. I kept my hand resting on him, unable to *not* touch him, still barely able to believe that he was alive, that what I had seen was real.

"I didn't lose you," I gulped.

He moved his head toward me, his lips resting against my forehead. They were warm. We stood there, our arms wrapped around one another, unable to talk. His touch was more like a blessing than a kiss. I closed my eyes, focusing on his regular heartbeat matching mine, my fingertips pressed against his bare skin.

Thank you, I whispered to whatever higher power was listening, *thank you.*

HAZEL

I felt like my body was being washed across an ocean, weightless, my bones like jelly and my mind drifting off without an anchor. I was dimly aware of Tejus calling down to me, and the walls of white light flickering past. He was carrying me, which explained why I felt weightless, but I could barely feel his arms around me. Whatever we had done, the barrier that we'd managed to create felt like it had taken every last cell of energy in my body. While we were creating it, I'd felt power running through my veins with such force I'd been afraid that I couldn't take it—but as soon as it stopped, it was like a bulb had exploded, the fuse dead. I had nothing left.

"Hazel, syphon off me!" Tejus barked out his order.

I wanted to tell him that I didn't think I *could*, that I just didn't feel like I had the energy to even attempt it, but the words just wouldn't form. All I wanted to do was sleep—sleep forever.

"Open the barrier!" Tejus called out to the waiting guards as we neared the palace.

We must have been the last to leave the battle. I couldn't remember who had been behind us as we created the white light—perhaps no one—but I could have sworn that I felt the flickers of an energy source that didn't belong to Tejus or me. But perhaps it had been my imagination. The whole thing felt like a strange dream anyway, one that I didn't have the energy to understand.

The white walls that had flamed up on either side of the path faded from view. I recognized the lawns of Memenion's palace, and saw the hordes of guards and sentries ambling around their tents. Cries from the wounded could be heard, and a hushed, respectful silence. We had lost many fighters in the hours before dawn.

"Put me down, Tejus," I whispered.

I didn't want my parents to see me cradled in his arms—they would think that I'd been hurt badly. He ignored me, but slowed his pace down from a run to a brisk walk.

"Please, Tejus. My parents. They'll worry."

He nodded curtly, gently helping me to my feet. His hands brushed along my sides as he checked for wounds, his eyes roving over my body. He was bleeding in a few places, but I was relieved to see the cuts were light—just flesh wounds and nothing more. Somehow, we had made it out of that battle alive.

"Ash!" I exclaimed, suddenly recalling his injury and Ruby riding off with him on the bull-horse.

Tejus shook his head.

"I haven't seen either of them. Ruby would have gotten him to safety though, don't worry."

His voice was coaxing and soft. I got the impression that he was telling me what I wanted to hear, not what he actually thought. I nodded, numbed. I couldn't even begin to imagine what Ruby would be going through right now.

"Hazel!"

My mom cried out my name. In an instant, she and my dad were standing next to me, Mom's eyes running over my body like Tejus's had to check that I wasn't harmed. When she was satisfied, she pulled me into a tight embrace.

Then it happened—the leap of hunger jumping up inside my chest.

"Mom," I breathed, firmly untangling myself.

"Are you hungry?" she asked, her eyes wide with concern.

"Hazel?" Tejus questioned. Their eyes were all fixed on me.

"It's fine, Hazel." My dad broke the pause. "Feed off me, I'm good to go."

I shook my head, trying to repel their energy from floating

my way. They all felt so *good*.

"I can't. There must be someone else, like a sentry?" I asked Tejus hopefully.

"Your parents would be better," he insisted.

"Hazel, please. If you need the energy, take it. You look like you can hardly walk," my dad agreed.

"Thank you," I whispered quietly. I felt so bad taking what little he had. We had all been in the battle—the fact that I felt so weak irritated me. Tejus seemed okay; I could sense his energy. It wasn't fully back to normal, but it seemed more robust than mine did.

My dad rested his hands on my shoulders.

"Feed," he urged.

I let my hunger satisfy itself, drawing his energy toward me, being as gentle as I could. I kept watching my dad's face as I syphoned, making sure I wasn't hurting him. He grinned at me, his brown eyes warm. Like the time I'd taken Mom's energy when we were building the barriers, I felt a glow of love emanating from my dad. His emotions felt more restless than hers, like half his mind was still on the battle, but I couldn't deny the fact that he was glad to be providing for me—happy to give me everything that he could.

It didn't take long for my body to return to normal. Clarity returned, and I felt like I'd woken, refreshed, from a deep sleep. I didn't have the jittery sensation that I got when I took too much, and I took that as a signal to stop, releasing the bond between us.

"Thanks, Dad," I muttered.

"Now can I yell at you for not doing what you were told?" he asked.

"You can!" my mom exclaimed, but took over anyway. "Hazel, you were told to move to the back of the ranks when things got dangerous, but you completely ignored us! Then you *ran* back to Tejus when you were commanded to get out of there!"

"I'm sorry," I groaned. There was no way they were going to make me regret or feel guilty for what I'd done. Tejus was standing, safe and alive, next to me—all because I'd refused to leave him behind. Not only that, but somehow we'd created a barrier that was more powerful than anything I'd seen before.

"Your parents are right," Tejus snapped. "You can't risk your life like that, Hazel. If something had happened…" His voice trailed off, his expression murderous.

Great. Now I was getting lectures from my boyfriend too?

"Mom, Dad." I turned to my parents, hoping to pacify them. "You sent me to Murkbeech to learn survival skills, right? And I've learned them—not in the way you wanted, but you need to let me use them. You need to *trust* me. I know you're worried constantly about Benedict and me, but we're okay. So far, we're okay."

My mom rubbed her temples. "I know," she sighed. "But there's no manual for this stuff, Hazel. You're still my child. I'm going to worry about you for eternity and then some. I will never be okay with you deliberately putting yourself in danger."

"And I won't do it again," I vowed, crossing my fingers behind my back.

She arched an eyebrow.

"You will," she replied, her lips pursing. "But I suppose I can't stop you."

She looked up at Tejus. It was a fleeting look, but I recognized the unspoken implication. Tejus was also to make sure I stayed safe—apparently, my staying alive was now his responsibility too, as far as she was concerned. I knew Tejus wouldn't argue with that—it seemed to have been his primary goal ever since he kidnapped me. In mom terms, that was acceptance into the family. I rolled my eyes, simultaneously annoyed that clearly no one believed I was capable of looking after myself, and secretly pleased that Mom and Dad were warming to Tejus.

"Tejus?" my grandpa Derek called, and I grinned.

Perfect timing.

"What was that?" he asked as he approached, looking from me to Tejus and back again, impatiently waiting for an answer.

"I have no idea." Tejus shook his head in bafflement. "I've never seen anything like it in my life. My only theory is that our weapons may somehow have helped us, being infused with the waters…but still. That much energy…"

"Can you try to recreate it around the palace?" my grandpa asked.

"We can," Tejus replied, "but not right now. Hazel needs to rest—it took a lot out of us both. I'm wondering if the extra energy came from us somehow syphoning off the rest of the army by mistake…or because we were all sharing energy, it created a build-up of some sort. I can't tell."

I was interested in Tejus's theories. Perhaps the energy that I hadn't recognized in our bond was an amalgamation of everyone else's? I couldn't imagine it coming from a singular source— Ash, Ruby and I had mind-melded together, and it hadn't produced results *close* to that.

"We should also go looking for Ruby and Ash," I interrupted. I wanted my friends safe before we attempted to try the barrier again—before we did *anything*.

Tejus turned to me in surprise. "Absolutely not."

What?

"Hazel, we're not going out to search for them. It's too dangerous," he replied firmly. "I'll send out some guards shortly—but you're not going with them."

"Ruby wouldn't leave me behind!" I exclaimed. "We have to get them, Tejus. We can't leave them out there alone."

"Don't worry." A hand was placed on my shoulder and I spun

around to see Claudia and Yuri standing behind me. I hadn't even heard them approach.

"We're going to go and look for them—they've gone to the Impartial Ministers' monastery. We can get there quickly on our own." Claudia's face was grim with determination.

"And Ash…" I hesitated, not sure if I should ask.

"If he needs the vampire transformation to stay alive, then I will happily give it," she confirmed.

"Claudia, careful. We don't know if the sentries can withstand the change," my grandpa reminded her.

"If it's his only chance, then we have to try it," Yuri replied.

"And have him go through the transformation while we're at war?" my mom asked quietly.

Claudia nodded.

"It's for Ruby. We have to try everything we can."

I was glad to hear that Claudia and Yuri were both willing to turn Ash if it came down to it. I knew that my best friend's happiness depended on Ash staying alive—whatever form that happened to be in.

I squeezed Claudia's hand, an unspoken gesture of gratitude. The woman nodded, and a second later Mona had joined them, and they were gone.

BEN

I held River's hand under the banquet table. She smiled at me, both of us glad the other was safe, along with Grace, Lawrence and, hopefully, Field. Our family had made it through the battle in one piece, and though there wasn't much about this morning I was grateful for, that was the one thing that mattered to me more than anything.

Reluctantly turning away from River, I looked around the room. GASP, Tejus, Queen Memenion and a few other ministers, including the aged Impartial Ministers, had assembled to discuss our next steps.

"The first thing we need to understand is what those creatures are—or at least what the entity actually is."

My voice cut through the mumbles of conversation that had broken out across the table. Everyone turned to me with varying degrees of blankness.

"The Elders are the closest comparison I can make," my father replied. "Clearly the entity's taken Tejus's brother's body and held him under possession in a similar way it did with Benedict."

"This is much stronger though," Tejus said. "When Benedict was under the possession of the entity, he never attempted to harm us directly—he was consumed by his mission to collect the stones. Jenus seems to be fully instated with the entity's physical strength."

"Benedict had moments of clarity, didn't he?" my dad asked.

Tejus nodded. "During the day."

"He was completely himself," Hazel added. "And confused about what he'd done the night before—he could remember certain bits, but not the full picture."

"It would be interesting to see if Jenus is affected the same way," I replied. "If he had moments of lucidity, it might mean that the entity is weak at that point."

"That could be the case," Tejus replied slowly, "but judging by what Benedict and the others saw at the cove, and Jenus's power, I wonder if this change is more permanent."

I was worried that Tejus was right, that the seemingly unbeatable strength and resilience of his brother couldn't be compromised in any way—not even with our weapons. The only saving grace was that they were at least effective against his armies…but even then, there seemed to be an unlimited supply of ashen-faced forms that had emerged from the black mists.

"Do you know anything that might be able to help us?" my grandfather, Aiden, growled at the Impartial Ministers, who were seated silently at the table, their eyes downcast as if they wished they could disappear.

One of them looked up, shaking his head.

"All we know is that whatever those creatures are, they were the first to inhabit Nevertide. Nothing more is said of them in our history books—we have searched, but each time it's proven to be fruitless."

I sighed inwardly, frustrated by the inability of the old men to come up with answers. It was looking like our only hope was my adopted son Field, my nephew Benedict, and the others—their success in finding the jinni or jinn they sought out, the only creatures of this land who would know anything.

"We need to see what's beyond Nevertide's waters," I announced. "There might be other supernatural communities that are familiar with the history of this land." I looked at Tejus, who was frowning. Queen Memenion was shaking her head—clearly she too was under the impression that Nevertide was alone in this dimension. That they were so isolated from the rest of the supernatural world that they'd never come across *any* of our kind before amazed me.

"I know you say there's nothing out there, but that can't possibly be true. We're in the supernatural dimension. Nevertide must *somehow* be connected to other lands. They might be at some distance, but we need to search."

After a brief pause, Tejus nodded his agreement, raking a palm across his brow. I respected the sentry, I understood that he—like most rulers or commanders—was proud, but he went up in my estimation in admitting that his world view might have been incorrect. It wasn't an easy admission to make.

"I agree," Ibrahim replied. "Corrine and I, along with some other witches, will investigate the waters. I presume there are safer ways to reach the borders of this land than the cove?"

"I would suggest heading to the Seraq kingdom. The rest of the coves are surrounded by forest," Tejus replied. "The palace is empty; I think her people have scattered. Take a few sentry guards with you to show you the way. The palace overlooks a cliff edge, down into the waters."

Ibrahim thanked him.

"We'll help secure the borders around the palace and then be on our way," the warlock informed us.

"We also need to find a way to close the portal," Sherus announced. "The entity and the shadow haven't left that location—there must be a reason. Perhaps it's the most convenient way for them to get to Earth? I don't know—what I *do* know is that the portal is important to them. When I left the battlefield, the shadow was hovering over the portal. Whether it was more of the creatures coming in, or them leaving, I couldn't be sure…but at the moment, we're leaving Earth exposed to attack."

The Impartial Ministers grumbled, no doubt more concerned with the fate of Nevertide than Earth. I *really* disliked those guys. Ignoring them, I turned to my father.

"I agree," he replied. "But first we need to ensure that we're safe here—then we'll send out a group to see if we can close it."

The fae king looked as if he was about to protest. I knew that he believed if the creatures could get to Earth, then they would also find a way to the In-Between.

My father silenced him with a raised hand. "Sherus, we lost many men today. We can't send more down to the cove till they've had time to recuperate. Let's hope that the entity is more intent on destroying us than anything else—so far that seems to be the case."

Lidera, Sherus's sister, placed a hand over her brother's.

"I agree with Derek," she replied quietly. "Let us deal with the immediate danger and wait until we hear back from the witches and warlock. The more we know, the better prepared we'll be to defeat the entity. At the moment, we're at a disadvantage. We were defeated today," she reminded him.

Sherus didn't say another word, but his face darkened. I felt compassion for the king—felt linked with him in a way that was hard to describe—and for his dimension. I worried about the fae kingdoms too. It was Sherus who had warned us of this threat, and I believed that the entity would come looking for the fae eventually—otherwise why would the king be the one to have experienced those omens? Still, Nevertide and the safety of GASP and the sentries had to be our priority. If we were defeated, then all hopes of Earth surviving an attack would be gone.

"We have one defense that appears to be able to halt the entity," I said, moving the discussion on as I turned to Hazel and Tejus. My niece looked worried for a moment.

"I don't know how we did it though, or even what it was," she replied doubtfully. "I'm not entirely sure we're going to be able to do it again."

"We can try," Tejus replied, looking at Hazel only. "When you're ready."

She nodded, her face still pale. I realized that her concern was the responsibility—if we all thought the barrier she and Tejus created was our only chance of survival, then a lot fell on their shoulders.

My sister and mother both instantly understood her reticence.

"Hazel, even if you can't do it again, it's fine. We'll find other ways to protect ourselves. There's usually more than one way to fight off a creature, no matter how powerful," Rose said.

Hazel bit her lip. "It's not just that though, is it?" she replied. "A barrier is one thing, but if we can find a way to harness that energy, it would also become our most effective *weapon*."

I tried to hide a smile as a bubble of pride welled up inside of me. I caught Caleb's eye. My niece was a born GASP member—a relatively short time spent in a supernatural dimension and she was already battle-strategizing like a pro.

"Exactly," my father replied, smiling at his granddaughter.

The pressure on my niece and her boyfriend to deliver was back on.

Julian

We traveled through endless forest, seeing nothing but the gray and brown barks of huge, ancient trees and their leafy branches. I had started to wonder if we were making any progress at all. After the incident with the goblins, we hadn't come across any other creatures, but a near-constant rustling in the undergrowth in the distance kept us all on edge.

I kept plodding along, not really interested in joining Benedict and Yelena's bickering. I supposed it kept them both distracted, but I couldn't concentrate on much other than the battle. I was worried about my parents and Jenney—and Ruby, Ash and Hazel. All of them. Their faces kept flashing though my mind, quickly being replaced by my memories of the shadow and the ashen figures that appeared from it.

I shuddered, trying to direct my focus on the journey.

As we progressed, the land slowly started to become stranger. The trees remained a constant, but soon bizarre-looking plants appeared, and muddy bogs that burped and bubbled, making me think of quicksand. I side-stepped them carefully, warning the others to do the same.

"How much further to the mountains?" Yelena grumbled.

Some luck she'd have in the marines.

"As long as it takes?" Benedict retorted irritably. "I don't know—Tejus didn't exactly include measurements in this half-assed map." He scrunched up the paper. It was pretty much redundant now anyway—none of the sentries had ventured this far into the forest. We'd just have to wait for the Hawk boys to come back and give us another vague 'we're almost there' answer.

"This is pixi-wagon!" I turned around at the sound of Aisha's voice. She was bent over a brightly colored purple flower.

"It's *what?*" Benedict asked.

"Pixi-wagon," Aisha replied dreamily. "My grandma used to grow this. She made perfume from it."

"Is it helpful?" I asked.

The jinni frowned at me.

"No, it's just nice. I haven't seen it for *years*." Suddenly she looked speculative, her fingers idly massaging the petal. "I had

BELLA FORREST

thought this mission was a babysitting job," she mused, "but actually, perhaps there *are* jinn in this land. Our kind used to breed these flowers."

"Glad to have you on board," Benedict replied grumpily.

Aisha rolled her eyes. "I didn't mean that—I just meant there's hope."

I was as annoyed as Benedict was at her admission that this was all a ruse to keep us away from harm, but I also took comfort from her words. If we could find the jinn or jinni who was behind the stones, then we would have a good chance of destroying the entity, or at least locking it up again for another eternity.

I picked up the pace. A few minutes later, the Hawk boys and Ridan came flying back down.

"This place is *weird*," Sky remarked as soon as his feet hit the ground. "I mean, weirder than the rest of Nevertide… We need to be careful, the ground gets rockier and more unstable the closer we get to the mountain range."

"Which is how far?" Benedict asked.

"Not that much further," came Fly's vague answer.

"Okay, but can you give us an actual estimate?" Benedict pressed. "Like, how many miles? One, fifteen, hundreds?"

The Hawk boys grinned, clearly amused by Benedict's irritation. Field took pity on him, playfully punching Sky in the arm.

35

"It's about twenty miles, give or take."

Twenty miles?

"We can carry you kids, if you like," Field replied, looking at our outraged expressions.

Aisha shook her head. "We don't know for sure the jinn are in the mountains. We need to check the forest too—and the best way to do that is on foot. The trees are too dense to see anything clearly."

"But we can't see more than a few feet into the forest anyway," I argued. "They could be a mile in that direction"—I pointed to our left—"and we'd never know about it!"

"Horatio and I would," Aisha insisted, glancing at her husband, who was still eyeing the pixi-wagon with a frown. "We can sense our kind, but it's more difficult if we're shooting through the air. We need to take this slow—it's the best chance we have of discovering them. I've got a feeling they're not going to want to be found."

"Okay." Benedict sighed. "I guess we keep walking then."

My shoulders slumped of their own accord. I was exhausted. The adrenaline surges over the past few days had been intense, and they had left me shattered.

"We'll return in a short while," Ridan replied. "You humans should eat something soon, though."

The dragon was right. The only problem was the quality of the food. I knew that in my backpack there were sandwiches made by Jenney—even the thought of what might be contained between the lumpy bread made my stomach turn over.

"We'll eat soon," Benedict replied, clearly no more eager than I was to discover the strange delights of Jenney's cooking.

We kept moving.

Soon I could see more light up ahead, the trees becoming less densely packed together and the wild undergrowth becoming sparser. As we got closer, I realized we were approaching a meadow. I moved faster, eager for a change of scenery and to see how far we were from the mountain range with my own eyes.

"Wow," I breathed. I had scrambled up on a fallen log to see the view. It didn't disappoint. No wonder the Hawk boys had described the land as 'weird'—I'd never seen anything like this before.

The meadow was huge, spreading for acres in each direction. I couldn't see the trees in the distance as the land rose in the middle, creating a large hill. Everywhere I looked I could see brightly colored flowers, a million different hues of color, and *bright*—like they were lit up from the inside.

I jumped down off the log and went to get a closer look. I could hear the others exclaiming as they followed me, then all racing down to the meadow.

The flowers mostly resembled the shape of poppies. They each had four rounded petals, with the stamen a darker, more intense color than the petals, which was where the mysterious light seemed to be emanating from.

"Careful!" Aisha called out. "Don't touch them!"

I drew back my hand. I'd been about to touch the center of the flower to see if the light was warm, or even real, but I realized the jinni was right. Touching flowers or any other plant in the supernatural world when you had no idea what it was wasn't a good idea.

"No, they're safe!" Benedict cried out, clutching one in his hand.

Of *course,* Benedict had gone ahead and picked one.

He had been running back toward me, but he stopped, standing still in the field, intently looking down at the flower in his hand.

"Benedict?" I was instantly worried. He could be such a *reckless id—*

He looked up and beamed at me. "These are like the stones!" he exclaimed. I stared at him in bewilderment. That admission didn't exactly make me feel comfortable.

"Put it down!" Yelena called out, her face horrified.

"No, you don't understand. I think they have energy in them," he called back, waving the flower about in excitement. "They're giving me the same feeling the stones did, like power entering my body."

He started to run toward us, and I bent down to inspect them more closely. I held my hand over the stamen, not wanting to touch it. After a while, I could see what he meant. It was like nothing I'd ever felt before—something strong and forceful moving up from my palm into the rest of me, making every nerve feel more *awake* somehow.

"See!" Benedict burst out jubilantly.

I looked around at the others. They were all starting to realize it too.

"I've never come across anything like this," Horatio muttered, still looking doubtful as to the safety of the plants. "They are powerful though… I can sense that."

Simultaneously, he and Aisha raised their hands over the bed of flowers nearest to them, falling silent, their eyes closed. We watched, waiting for their verdict.

Eventually, Aisha turned to us. She shrugged.

"They seem safe… The energy is pure, natural, and I can't detect the magic of any other supernatural creature on them."

"Me neither," Horatio replied.

I heard the flapping of wings above us, and the Hawk boys landed in the field along with Ridan.

"Isn't it crazy?" Fly grinned. "This place must look amazing at night. I wonder why the sentries never knew it was here?"

"We don't know that they didn't—they might know all about it," I replied.

Benedict looked doubtful. "An entire field of energy-providing plants? They would have mentioned it—every contender in the trials would have been up here. *And,*" he continued, pacing the meadow in excitement, "we'd see them everywhere—they would have planted more."

"Then this is great!" Yelena cried gleefully. "We can send these back to them. All the sentries can get help healing after the battle!"

The energy levels of Benedict and Yelena seemed to be skyrocketing. They were the only two holding the plants.

"Guys, put them down," I interjected, "you're getting hyper. We don't know what exposure to these plants would do to *humans.*" I'd seen Benedict get like this before in Hawaii, when he'd downed six Coca-Colas in a row as a dare.

Benedict went red, and dropped the flower.

"But the idea is great," I continued hastily. "We should get the flowers to the sentries—as quickly as we can. Either it's going to help heal the wounded, or it's going to help them while they battle."

Aisha nodded. "Ridan, Field, Fly, and Sky; you should help Horatio and me pick as many as we can." She turned to the three of us humans. "You avoid them and start making your way to the other edge of the meadow. Horatio and I will meet you there when we're done. The Hawks can deliver them."

"Yeah," Benedict said, "good idea, Aisha."

We made our way across the meadow, and I smiled to myself for the first time in a while. I hoped that the flowers we'd found here might make a difference to the outcome of the battle, or at least help the sentries when they returned. Not only that, it would help GASP too. Derek had been astounded when Tejus and Ash had told him he just needed to wait after syphoning for his energy to return…these flowers could change all that. The sentries could syphon off the GASP members as much as they liked, and it wouldn't make a difference.

I glanced over at Benedict. He was grinning from ear to ear.

"We're going to be heroes, right?" I said, nudging him.

"Heck, yeah."

"Even more so if we find the jinn," I added.

"They'll probably make us honorable dignitaries of Nevertide or something," Benedict replied.

"Or we'd get statues."

"Maybe we'd get our own *vultures?*" he mused, his eyes gleaming.

"Kingdoms even—it's not like they have many rulers left!"

Yelena tutted and rolled her eyes in disgust.

RUBY

Ash climbed out of the pool first. When I approached the side to do the same, I was surprised when he gripped my waist, lifting me out easily. Clearly it wasn't just Ash's wound that was healed—his whole body appeared to have been infused with energy, just like the weapons had been.

"How are you feeling?" I asked.

"Amazing, actually," Ash replied, looking confused. "Better than I ever have. A bit like I've never expended an ounce of energy in my *life*. Do you feel any different?"

I ran a mental check down my body, but in all honesty, I felt far from okay. My muscle ache had eased off a bit since being in the water, but mentally I was exhausted.

I shook my head, smiling. "I think all the water magic went to you—I feel like I could sleep for a month."

Suddenly, Ash's expression changed. He was looking over at the other side of the chamber, and I turned to follow his gaze. I couldn't see anything.

"True Sight?" I asked.

"Yeah." He nodded. "We have company."

It took a while, but eventually three of the Impartial Ministers came into view. I suspected, though couldn't be sure, that these were the same three we'd left in the immortal waters when we'd taken the others back to the palace.

"What do you think they want?" I hissed at Ash.

"No idea…though I suspect we're in some kind of trouble."

I scoffed. If one of them even mentioned the fact that only Impartial Ministers were privy to the waters, I would drown them in there myself.

"Easy." Ash smirked at me. My fury must have been obvious. I smiled at him sheepishly, waiting for them to approach.

"Emperor of Nevertide," one of them called out, his voice sounding like the crumbling of dry leaves. These guys were so *old*—perhaps even more ancient than the two back at Memenion's palace.

"Welcome to the brotherhood of the Impartial Ministers." Another one greeted him with a small nod of his head.

I looked up at Ash, confused.

What the heck does that mean?

They came closer, their cataract-ridden eyes taking us both in. I stared back, trying once again to guess how old they might actually be. Centuries old? Or was it millennia?

"Who would have thought, the kitchen king made emperor, joining our kind," said the third. His tone was far crueler than the others, his lip curled up in a sneer. Instantly, I was on the defensive—kitchen king? Ash was the one saving their kind from complete destruction!

"What are you talking about?" I snapped.

"Emperor Ashbik has been healed by the waters of *Immortalitatem.* Those blessed by its powers are capable of living many lifetimes," the first minister replied, "thus joining our brotherhood and becoming an Impartial Minister—those, like us, who have lived so long we have no vested interest in the outcome of Nevertide's politics, and so remain impartial, able to teach lesser men."

I burst out in laughter at the old man's statement.

"No vested interest?" I scoffed. "What about your support of Queen Trina? How you denied that she'd killed Hadalix, and supported her rise to power?"

All three of the men glowered at me.

I didn't care—it wasn't like I was looking for their approval, and any vague respect I'd had for them in the beginning, more due to their age than anything else, was rapidly vanishing. They were relics of a past that no longer had any role here. They had gotten crusty and arrogant, thinking that they could control the future of Nevertide through manipulation and game-playing. With the rise of the entity and its army, their time was over.

"We did what we thought was best," the first minister replied. I'd heard it all before.

"I'm not interested in joining your *brotherhood*," Ash replied coldly. "I have a vested interest in the outcome of Nevertide, and I hope I always will. If we survive this war, that's how this land will be run in the future—by people who care. Lock yourselves away in this monastery if you want, hoping that the entity won't find you, but your time of power and influence is over."

The Impartial Ministers looked affronted. The third looked furious—his face darkened and his staff trembled in his hand.

"If we don't have a role here, Nevertide will not last long," he spat.

"We'll see about that," Ash replied levelly. "Come on, Ruby—we need to get out of here."

We walked away from them, but I could feel their glares resting on our departing figures. I was glad to be out of there, but I wanted answers. What did it mean that Ash would now live many lifetimes? Was he immortal now, or was that only if he continued to use the waters in the same way that the ministers did?

"Ash," I whispered before we left, "don't you think we need

more information on what just happened? The waters obviously changed you somehow—"

"Don't worry," he replied swiftly. "We can talk to the other ministers when we get back. I'm not interested in talking to them, and I don't trust them to tell me the truth. Not really."

"Okay," I replied. I wondered if it was pride getting in the way of Ash asking them questions. I understood if it was—the disdain they felt toward him was obvious. I just hoped he *would* seek out the answers when we got back to the palace. If my fiancé was suddenly immortal, I wanted to know about it.

We started making our way back down the narrow passage, following the trail of blood that we'd made on our way in.

"Guess I was injured pretty badly," Ash commented dryly.

I nodded. I wasn't ready to joke about it. I half wanted to scream that he'd nearly *died* on me—it wasn't something I'd get over any time soon.

He paused in the passage, turning around to face me.

"Ruby, are you okay?" he asked.

No.

I tried to smile reassuringly up at him, but I faltered.

"That was the most terrifying couple of hours of my life…I thought you weren't going to make it." My voice had come out raspy and high-pitched, and I squeezed my hands into fists, embarrassed that I wasn't holding myself together, knowing that *he'd* been the one injured and at death's door, not me.

He moved his hand to my cheek, wiping away a tear I hadn't even realized had fallen.

"I'm so sorry. I didn't realize," he whispered.

"You don't need to be sorry," I replied. "You were the one hurt! I just—it was scary, that's all. I'll be all right in a minute."

"You don't have to be all right, Shortie. You've been through a lot—we both have."

I nodded, brushing away my tears hastily. They kept falling down my face, not caring that I was commanding them to stop.

"If our roles had been reversed," he continued, "I don't know what I would have done, so don't get angry at yourself for being scared. I would have been terrified—I was. When the creature ripped through me and I fell to the ground, my only thought was that I wasn't going to be able to protect you, and that image came into my mind—from the mind-meld, you standing at the door of our house, with your baby bump. The thought that we wouldn't get that—the thought that we wouldn't get our future together—that pain was worse than anything the creature could have done to me."

He held me close, and I buried my head in his chest. His words were comforting. I realized that I wasn't alone in this. Ash was safe. I was safe. Our survival was all that truly mattered to me right now. Even though everything else felt uncertain, my feelings for Ash weren't—they were the one thing that I could cling onto, no matter what was coming our way.

"Thank you," I whispered, smiling up at him, a genuine smile this time.

"Are you ready to face your parents and Mona?" he asked.

"What?"

"They've just arrived," he replied, nodding his head in the direction of the valley.

We made our way out of the passage, coming face to face with Mona and my mom and dad, waiting by our bull-horse. They'd obviously heard us coming, as I could see the relief on all of their faces.

"Ugh! Thank *God* you're okay!" My mom enveloped me in a fierce embrace, and then moved to let my dad do the same. "And you, Ash—how are you feeling?" my mom asked with concern, her eyes darting over his miraculously healed wound.

"Better than I've ever felt, to be honest."

"The water worked then?" my dad asked, also staring at Ash's unblemished chest.

"Impressive," Mona murmured.

My mom turned to Ash, clearly shocked at his swift recovery. "I guess there's no need to turn you then."

Mom!

Ash instinctively took a step back, his expression horrified. I rolled my eyes.

"That wasn't really an option," I reassured him hastily.

Ash nodded mutely, his gaze zoning in on my mom and dad's teeth.

"Let's get going," I sighed.

ASH

A vampire?

Was that what Ruby's mother meant?

I didn't really understand the logistics of it, but I'd heard Ruby mention the phrase 'to turn' when she was explaining GASP to me, and the supernatural nature of her family. Partly, I was flattered—I'd wanted Ruby's family to accept me, and I supposed you couldn't ask for more acceptance than an offer that loosely translated into, 'Hey, come and be part of the family for eternity.' But I didn't know how sold I was on vampirism. Obviously, there were benefits—the speed, the strength and the immortality—I guessed that was a double-edged sword, and one that I might just have been gifted anyway, if the Impartial

Ministers were to be believed…I wasn't entirely convinced that they were.

The concept of 'turning' was a lot to digest. I still didn't understand the transformation process, and wasn't even sure that sentries could be turned—though the GASP organization certainly contained a lot of supernatural cross-breeds like the half-Hawks and human-fae. I supposed I would have time later to consider this, and it would be something that Ruby would have to decide as well. She'd made no secret of her ambition to eventually join her vampire clan, and I didn't want to dissuade her…but I'd never for a moment considered joining her in the transformation.

I shoved the thought aside and tried to compose myself. I didn't want Ruby thinking that the idea shocked me too badly, and I didn't want to cause her family offense. Plus, we had more pressing matters to attend to.

"What happened in the battle?" I asked as we prepared to depart.

Claudia sighed and Yuri and the witch looked downcast. Whatever the news was, it wasn't good. I'd thought because all three of them had taken the time to come and find us, everything might have gone well. Clearly not.

"There were quite a few casualties," Yuri replied. "We couldn't defeat the shadow—or the entity. We've retreated back to the palace."

"The only good news is the barrier," Claudia interjected. "Something that Hazel and Tejus made—none of us know how. But it was powerful enough to repel the shadow, and escape the entity."

I nodded, jumping up on the bull-horse with a heavy heart.

"How are they?" Ruby asked.

"Hazel and Tejus? They're fine. So are the rest of GASP."

Ruby nodded, still looking as despondent as I felt. I was glad that none of our friends had been injured, but a retreat wasn't good—and neither were the deaths of Nevertide's people.

"Let's go, Ruby." I held out my hand to pull her on to the bull-horse, and she clambered on in front of me.

"We can take the bull-horse too, if you want to come with us," Mona informed us. "But if you are going to ride, Tejus said to avoid the forests, stick to the main roads."

I nodded. There was no danger of me going anywhere *near* a forest.

I looked at Ruby, wondering which method of transport she'd prefer.

"Let's go with Mona. I want to get back as soon as possible."

I nodded, and we all formed a circle with the witch.

"Can we stop for a moment at the cove?" I asked. "Only if it's safe. I want to check the state of the portal."

The witch nodded, and a split-second later, we appeared on the main road, at a safe distance from the cove. Above the trees that blocked the shore from view, I could see the shadow. It remained in one spot—swaying in the breeze, but very determinedly hovering over the ocean.

"Look at it," Claudia murmured, gazing in the direction of the water.

"Why is it remaining there?" I breathed. "Everyone's at the palace, right? Why hasn't it continued to attack?"

"I just don't know," Yuri said. "The entity has all the power. The shadow would have annihilated us during the battle had it not been for Tejus and Hazel. But it must realize that Tejus and Hazel would be too weak to try the barrier again so soon—at least Jenus would realize that." Yuri shook his head in confusion and frustration.

I asked them both for details on the barrier. I'd never heard of such a thing happening before, and when they described it to me I was even more confused. The white light could definitely be attributed to the immortal waters and their weapons, but that much power? It seemed impossible that they could do such a thing.

Looking back in the direction we'd just traveled from, the sight of burnt-out farmhouses and land that poured into the earth depressed me. Even if we were to survive this, what hope did Nevertide have? How would it ever come back from this? We had a small fraction of the villagers from the five kingdoms at Memenion's palace. The others I presumed had scattered, perhaps hiding out in abandoned castles or seeking shelter in the remaining villages that were still standing. We hadn't come across any of the people from Seraq's kingdom—not ministers, guards or villagers. I wondered if they were still alive, or if they too had suffered at the hands of their queen.

It would take a lot of time and a lot of work to get the land back on its feet. I glanced over at Ruby. I hoped that she would eventually realize that Nevertide needed her as much as it needed me. When Tejus had made his speech before the battle about the loving queen they would receive, my heart had swelled with pride. I couldn't imagine anyone better suited to the job—if she was willing to take it.

"We need to get back to the palace," I muttered. "I don't think the shadow's going to remain above the portal forever. We'll be under attack again before we know it."

Claudia nodded. "I agree. And we're just as powerless as we were before—especially if Hazel and Tejus don't understand what they created. If they can't do it again, we're in trouble."

We gathered around Mona once again, and the cove vanished from view.

HAZEL

"This isn't going well," I sighed, dropping my arms down. The muscles in my biceps ached, and my head was pounding from the exertion. We'd only been trying for about an hour, but my mental energy was quickly depleting, even though I was syphoning off Tejus, at his request, while we worked.

"I know," he muttered. "I just don't understand it. What happened in the first place? How were we able to do something like that? Not knowing is making this all the more frustrating."

"Let's take a break." I gestured for him to sit down next to me. We were practicing in one of the more remote parts of Memenion's garden. The flowers and bushes were overgrown and overrun with weeds. I was perched on the edge of an old marble fountain. Its waters had long dried up, leaving green stains running down the image of a bird in mid-call, his beak where the spout was supposed to be.

Tejus wearily took a seat. I could see perspiration beading at his temples and along his shoulder blades and back. He was wearing a GASP tank provided by my great-grandfather Aiden—the material far more advanced than anything they had in this land, especially when it came to training and battle.

He reached out a hand and clasped mine tightly, his thumb moving in circular motions over my skin.

"We'll find a way, don't worry," he murmured. He moved my hand up to kiss it softly, his eyes fixed on some point in the distance ahead, distracted by something else.

"Do you think it was desperation?" I asked, trying to recall what had happened during the battle—anything that might help us better understand what led up to the creation of the wall. "As in life-or-death pressure—you know how people get adrenaline rushes and lift vehicles off babies, things like that?" I asked.

"Not specifically, no… I don't actually know exactly what you mean by *vehicles*, but I understand the gist. It could be that."

He looked doubtful, and to be honest, so was I. Adrenaline could have explained some of what happened—perhaps the intensity of the barrier, reaching all the way back to the castle— but it wouldn't explain all of it. Not the white light and how it was the only thing that the entity didn't seem to be able to overcome.

"And that energy from the other sentries," I mused, "do you think that explains it?"

"I'm not sure about that either. I've been in battles before—I haven't experienced anything coming close to our power surge. I'm starting to wonder if it's all *you*."

"What do you mean?" I asked, confused that he'd even consider that my 'baby' sentry powers could create something so radical.

"Well, you're the only unknown factor. A human-turned-sentry. Your energy has always been so potent. I wonder if you have additional abilities that haven't been explored yet."

I considered what he was saying. As much as I'd have *liked* to believe him, it didn't really ring true. I hadn't felt the power coming from me, or specifically from Tejus. As far as I could recall—and my memories of the event were hazy at best—in the moment, I'd felt like I was tapping into another energy source.

"I don't know, Tejus. It seems unlikely," I countered.

"Does it?" He turned to me, his eyes gleaming. "Sometimes I think that you're capable of anything—you've transformed me utterly, changed my entire world, just by being you."

He shifted on the edge of the fountain so his body was facing toward me. He placed a hand on my hip, moving me toward him.

"You're an unexpected miracle, Hazel Achilles," he breathed, moving a strand of hair that had fallen across my face. His dark eyes had grown blacker, the pupils dilating as he gazed down at me. Once again I was completely distracted, this time finding it difficult to breathe.

"Part of me wants to lock you away in a tower, never let you come to harm—never allow another being to so much as look upon you." He grazed my jaw with his thumb, moving our lips closer as he spoke. "The other part of me, the more rational part"—the corners of his mouth twitched up in wry amusement—"just wants to sit back and let you astound the world. To set you free from anything that might hold you back, myself included."

I shook my head. "You wouldn't hold me back. You know how to love better than you think you do."

My lips pressed against his. His mouth had a salty tang that drove me crazy. Our kiss deepened, driven by my urge to be as close and intimate with Tejus as I possibly could. My tiredness had completely vanished. I wished that I could freeze time—that this moment could last for an eternity, that our heated kiss would never have the chance to cool off.

"Are we interrupting something?"

Reluctantly I drew myself back from Tejus, and grinned at Ash and Ruby, who had entered through the arch in the garden wall. I couldn't believe that Ash was standing, let alone smirking at the two of us.

"Welcome back," Tejus announced dryly. He stood up, frowning at Ash—I could see he was just as amazed at our friend's transformation from nearly dead to healthy.

Ruby broke the strangeness of the moment by running forward and enveloping me in a massive hug. I returned it, grinning like a maniac—not just because I was profoundly relieved to see her alive and well, but also because the hunger that would have made me hesitate in the past was completely absent.

"Okay," I laughed, untangling myself. "What the hell happened? I saw your injuries, Ash—I didn't expect to see you on your feet for a while."

"I'm as amazed as you are. The immortal waters are even more impressive than I thought," he replied. "To be frank, I'm furious that the Impartial Ministers kept it to themselves—if we'd known about it..." His voice trailed off. I guessed where his thoughts were going—if the waters could heal him from an injury like that, then their medicinal properties could have helped a lot of sentries over the years.

"Let's just be thankful that Queen Trina wasn't aware of it," Tejus replied. "Or my father."

Tejus moved over to the overgrown lawn where we'd been practicing our barrier-building, and bent down to retrieve something from the ground. I recognized the Hellswan sword, enclosed in its protective sheath.

"This belongs to you." Tejus proffered the weapon in Ash's direction. "I picked it up when you were attacked. I hoped you'd be back to claim it."

Instead of taking it out of Tejus's hand, Ash crossed his arms and shook his head.

"The sword no longer belongs to me, Tejus. You're the remaining heir of the Hellswan family—and the kingdom is gone. You're its rightful owner."

Tejus cocked an eyebrow.

"It's good steel, Ash."

"It's more than that, and you know it."

Tejus paused for a moment, and then nodded his thanks. He reattached the sword to his belt. "Make sure you pick up another from the armory, today," he murmured. He seemed to be shrugging off the sentiment of the gift, but I knew Tejus better than that. He was deeply moved by Ash's actions.

Ruby winked at me, obviously thinking the same thing.

A moment later, my grandpa, great-grandpa Aiden, and Sherus walked into the garden. Their eyes lighted with surprise on Ash, and they made the same stunned remarks that Tejus and I had about his bizarrely good health.

"How's the barrier coming along?" my grandpa asked, once Ash had debriefed them all.

"Not well," Tejus replied curtly. "We'll keep trying, but I'm not holding out much hope. Until we know how it happened,

I'm not entirely sure we're going to be able to replicate it."

My grandpa nodded, but he and Sherus exchanged a worried glance. I felt terrible that I was letting them down—and we *would* keep trying, but it was starting to feel near impossible. I wondered how much time we had left before the entity and its army struck again. Shouldn't we be looking for another way to hold them off?

"We all need to get some rest," my grandpa announced. "We don't know when the next attack is going to be, and I advise that you try to recuperate while we have the chance."

"Are the ministers still working in shifts to maintain the barriers?" Tejus asked.

"They are," Aiden confirmed.

Before Tejus could say another word, Ibrahim and Corrine appeared from the opposite side of the garden, making their way toward us with perturbed expressions.

"Derek, there you are," Ibrahim called out, untangling his jacket from a thorn bush as they hurried toward us.

I waited impatiently for the witch and warlock to tell us what they'd found across the water. They sounded a little breathless as they approached—they'd obviously been looking for my grandpa for a while.

"It's blocked off," Ibrahim announced as soon as he reached us. "We can only get ten or so miles out to sea, then we can't go any further. There's some kind of dome over Nevertide."

"Can you see anything?" my grandpa asked.

Corrine shook her head.

"There's some kind of illusion on the barrier, or 'dome' — showing more sea until the horizon, then there's nothing but sky."

"Is it like a sentry barrier?" I asked, wondering if the Impartial Ministers were responsible for this as well.

"Not exactly," Ibrahim replied. "We never touched the surface of it exactly. It was like we were moving forward, but staying in the same place—more of a figurative barrier than a physical one."

"Actually, that sounds familiar," Ruby mused, "similar to the barrier that we faced when we tried to get out of Nevertide. But then we *did* touch the surface, and it stretched like elastic. Maybe it's different."

"There definitely wasn't anything we could touch in place— we tried. The illusion reaches upward as well, creating a shelter over the land. Whoever put it in place is exceptionally powerful—this isn't the work of sentries," Corrine said, glancing over at Ash and Tejus. Her eyebrows rose slightly as she saw Ash, but she didn't comment on his appearance.

"Are we thinking that the jinn or jinni created it?" Aiden asked.

The witches looked at one another, silently deliberating.

"We think so," Ibrahim replied slowly. "I can't think what

other creature would have the power to make something so impenetrable and impervious to other forms of magic, except perhaps the entity, but this dome has obviously been up for a long time. The entity wouldn't have been able to maintain it while locked in the stones. This kind of power requires a constant source."

"And what about the rips in the sky?" my grandpa asked. "Are they not breaks in the dome?"

"We thought so at first," Ibrahim replied, "and they certainly appear to be signs of the entity trying to break this barrier, or dome, but he hasn't succeeded." The warlock looked troubled, scratching his head before continuing. "It is strange... Almost as if the sky itself is an artifice which the entity has ripped, but not been able to break through."

"We recognized some of the constellations as we got closer though," Corrine added. "The sky is the same as that in the supernatural realm. There must be other lands outside of this one – we should consider this dome a blessing, in a way."

Everyone was silent as we digested the information. It just seemed so strange to me that there would be jinn living here who had gone undetected for so long. Especially if they had so much power over Nevertide—what was in it for them? Why did they so badly want to be cut off from the rest of the supernatural world—especially now, with the entity having escaped? Surely, at this moment, this was the most dangerous land in all the dimensions?

"I agree that this is good thing." Sherus broke the silence first, his voice low and thoughtful. "It means there's only one way out of Nevertide—through that portal. Which means there's only one location that we need to guard and protect. Whatever happens, the entity must not be permitted to leave."

I agreed with the fae king, but it was easier said than done. The entity was obviously aware of the fact, which was why it had chosen to concentrate its army at the cove. For all we knew, some of its army might have already escaped through the portal to Earth.

"We will find a way to shut it," Aiden replied, "but not until we find a way to distract the entity. We can't, and *won't*, just blindly send more men out there to die."

I could tell the fae king wanted to protest, but this operation was under GASP's control. We would just have to wait, patiently, till we got our opportunity…

I hoped it would be sooner rather than later.

HAZEL

I awoke with a start, sitting bolt upright in bed. It was still mid-afternoon, judging by the position of the sun, and the room was silent.

What woke me?

I looked over at Tejus. He was groaning in his sleep, his eyes screwed shut with an expression of anguish across his face. Without warning, he suddenly cried out, his muscles tensing, entwining his body in the covers.

"Tejus, Tejus, wake up—you're having a bad dream," I whispered, gently shaking him. He caught my wrist in a tight grip, holding it still. His eyes opened, staring up at me. It took a moment for the dream to pass and for reality to reassert itself—

eventually I could see his eyes focus, and he released my hand.

"Sorry," he gasped, sitting up in bed.

His body was drenched in sweat, and he sat for a moment, his head clasped in the palms of his hands.

"Are you okay?" he asked.

Am I okay?

"I'm fine! Wh-What happened?"

He shook his head, his hand coming to rest on the sheets, but his gaze was fixed ahead, as if he was reliving whatever it was he'd dreamed all over again.

"Tejus, stop," I said firmly. "You need to talk—what was that about? Was it the battle?"

He shook his head again.

"No," he replied quietly. "It wasn't the battle we were in—it was other…places. On Earth, and somewhere else. People screaming, running for their lives, panicking…there was nothing I could *do*."

My blood ran cold.

"Did it feel like it was a vision, or an omen?" I replied slowly.

"I don't know. Perhaps."

I reached out and touched his hand. He jumped a little, instinctively trying to move it away, but I held on, and eventually I felt his muscles relax.

"Can you share it through a mind-meld?" I asked. "Like we did when Queen Trina tried to kidnap me?"

"We could." He gulped. "It's not pleasant."

"All the more reason for me to see it. If it is a vision of some kind, then it would be good to know where on Earth these things are taking place."

"All right," he conceded. "Just tell me to stop when you've had enough."

I nodded.

"Promise me," he growled.

"I promise," I replied, hiding a smile. Tejus was trying to protect me from dreams now? He obviously hadn't realized the extent of my over-active imagination. If he didn't show me, I would imagine the worst.

I felt his energy reaching out for mine, dark and silken, like wisps of smoke. I realized that I was witnessing the look and *feel* of a nightmare. Instead of Tejus's normal golden threads of mental energy, they had been distorted by whatever had plagued his mind. Regardless, my own energy reached out and intertwined with his, and soon the room, the bed, and Tejus's form next to me faded away to nothingness. I felt like I was suspended in mid-air, surrounded by gray, ashen matter— almost as if I was in the midst of the shadow army itself.

The mists started to move, and suddenly I was jolted violently into a vision. I was on Earth, standing on a wide, neatly manicured lawn. Screams of terror came from behind me. Spinning around, I saw a multitude of people running at me head-on. Men with briefcases, women holding strollers and small children, students with book bags, and waiters still wearing aprons—hundreds of them all yelling and crying. I looked up to the sky, seeing the shadow of the entity appearing over a large, steel structure. Before I could react, a woman barged past me. As our eyes met, her body transformed, her blue dress and pretty face becoming distorted, graying before my eyes, till her sockets were black holes and she roared at me, her jaw hanging as the shadow consumed her. I screamed, feeling a burning sensation at the back of my mouth.

The vision vanished just as abruptly as it had come, and I was jolted to a new destination—another place on Earth, with cobbled streets and small, pretty shop windows that were twinkling. I could smell the aroma of chocolate, and hear a bell sounding in the distance. The screams sounded again, and I could hear the echo of hundreds of people running a few streets away, the shop windows shaking from the stampede.

Before I could even witness the horror of the people, I was transported again—this time to a more metropolitan destination that I recognized as London. I was by the River Thames, looking out toward Big Ben. The shadow slowly moved toward me, darkening the buildings like a huge thundercloud. A single cry went up, and I looked over to the left, watching a child crying over a fallen ice-cream. The ground started to shake beneath my feet. The child's mother looked up, her gaze confused, then quickly turning to fear as the earth jolted.

I turned my head back toward the shadow, but it was too late. I was already being shown another vision, another city—this one I didn't recognize immediately, but it was just as crowded as the one before. Now the vision was starting to flicker and blur, and I thought my time in Tejus's head was up.

I could feel our bond weakening, but before it did I saw another place, certainly *not* on Earth. This one was impossibly beautiful, with a large white-stone fortress in front of me, and leaping ice-fire fountains marking the way to the door of the castle. I heard a roar—loud and inhuman, one that shook my bones, making my entire body tremble. I shut my eyes against it, not wanting to see anymore. The next moment, I was back in the room, pushing Tejus away from me.

"That was horrible," I rasped, leaping up from the bed.

"I know," he replied quietly.

I realized why he hadn't wanted to share it with me. It wasn't what I'd seen exactly that was so terrifying, though that was bad enough, but more what I'd *felt*. I'd been so helpless to do anything except acknowledge the crushing force of the entity— knowing, with every fiber of my being, that it was coming, but that I would be able to do nothing. That we had already lost.

"It's showing us, isn't it? It's showing us how powerful it is. That... that we're already too late?" I stammered my question to Tejus, my heart beating erratically. I paced up and down the room, my arms clutched tight around my frame.

"Hazel, stop." Tejus threw back the covers. "Get back into bed. You need to calm down; this isn't helping anyone."

His words felt harsh, but he was right—I was starting to get hysterical and panic. I took a deep breath, trying to regulate my heartbeat. I walked slowly back to the bed, and climbed in. Tejus drew me next to him.

"We'll go down and speak to Derek in a minute," he assured me.

His arms wrapped around me, and I lay with my head against his chest. He felt so solid and comforting, further aiding my return to reality.

"I recognized some of those places," I whispered. "London, Paris—that was the one with the lawns and the big tower in the distance—and I think one of them was on a planet in the In-Between. Something about it reminded me of the fae…but I'm not sure what, exactly."

"Will the others know?" he asked.

"Yeah, I think so. Most of GASP have traveled the world over. I just hope I can describe them well enough—the visions are so disjointed."

Tejus was silent, his fingers methodically running down the length of my hair.

"If they are visions, and they come from the entity, why is it showing them to us?" he mused, sighing.

"I guess to taunt us? They had that kind of feel to them, like the powerlessness—I got the impression we were being shown something we couldn't stop."

"Did you feel anything else—like an energy…that didn't belong to you or me?" he asked tentatively.

"Do you mean the same as when we built the barrier? I don't know—it was strange, but I put that down to being a nightmare, of sorts."

He fell silent again, and I wondered what he was thinking.

"You're right," he agreed eventually, "it was probably that. Let's go and speak to your grandfather. We need to warn the rest of them."

I slid off the bed, with some reluctance. I got the impression that Tejus was holding something back from me—a thought or idea. I didn't push him though. He was right. GASP needed to know what was coming.

BENEDICT

When we reached the end of the poppy field, there was more forest waiting for us. I groaned inwardly. I'd had enough of battling my way through trees and brambles and narrowly avoiding falling into bogs. I could see why none of the sentries ventured up here. If the creatures weren't going to get you, then the plants probably would.

"More forest?" Yelena moaned. "Ugh. I'm *sick* of forest."

"We know the mountains aren't far now," Julian replied, but he sounded just as weary as the rest of us – the energy from the flowers had drained quickly. The end did seem to be in sight though. Now, when we looked up, we could see the peaks of the mountains through the tree branches in the distance—but at least they were in sight.

"So then we're going to have to scale that massive thing?" Yelena whined.

"Do you have any better ideas?" I retorted.

"I do—we can at least rest and eat something, and I can get rid of the pebble in my boot that's been driving me crazy for the last three miles."

I looked over at Julian, who shrugged.

"Okay," I replied, "let's wait for Horatio and Aisha, and then we can stop for a bit."

A split second later, the jinni couple joined us. Ridan had flown on ahead already, making sure no danger lurked in wait.

Aisha surveyed the forest. "Horatio and I should span out," she announced. "This seems to be the densest past of the forest, an ideal location to hide, and the pixi-wagon gives me reason to think that jinn may be nearby. If you head north," she looked at all three of us, "Horatio and I will go east and west, we'll cover more ground that way. Call us if you see anything – or if you sense danger. We'll hear you."

I nodded in agreement, not wanting to bring up the subject of us having a rest. There would be time enough for that when we found what we were looking for.

"Be cautious," Horatio murmured, raising his brows in warning. The next moment, the couple had vanished, and we were left to walk ahead.

Yelena started whining again almost instantly. After I snapped at her, she huffed something under her breath and marched on ahead. I wanted to tell her to stop stomping about—she was only advertising to the rest of the forest that we were approaching.

"Let her be," Julian said, before I could open my mouth.

"That much noise and her blaze of red hair? She's like a police siren," I muttered.

"I don't think there's much around here that's interested in harming us—they would have hunted us down already."

I looked about at the new stretch of forest. I wasn't so sure that Julian was correct. This part seemed even gloomier than the last. Thick mists settled along the floor, and the place was totally silent—no birds, no rustling in the undergrowth. Nothing. The temperature seemed to have dropped as well. I shrugged off my backpack and pulled out another robe to wear.

"We'll get warmer as we move," Julian pointed out.

"Yeah, but it's damp too—can't you feel it?"

He didn't reply, but started moving faster, trying to shake off the chill. I followed him, using my walking stick to feel the steps ahead. In some parts the mists were so dense I couldn't see the forest floor.

"Aghhhhhhh!"

I heard Yelena scream.

"Yelena!" I called out, running forward with Julian, forgetting to use the stick. We didn't hear another sound from her, and I started to *really* panic.

"We're coming!" I yelled, moving as fast as I could without falling flat on my face. I was about to take another step when Julian yanked me back.

"Hey!"

I stopped. He'd been more cautious and seen what I couldn't. We were standing in front of a massive pit, our feet inches from the edge. I peered down, trying to see beyond the mists that had covered it from view. Sure enough, I could see a flicker of red hair at the bottom.

"I think I twisted my ankle," Yelena cried pitifully.

I groaned. "Okay," I called. "We're coming to get you."

I looked at Julian. He was scratching his head, trying to work out how we were going to get down without falling in ourselves.

"Over there?" I pointed to the edge that looked the least steep.

"Hmm… Looks pretty slippery. Maybe we should just call for Aisha and Horatio?"

"Good point," I sighed. Cupping my hands around my mouth, I started to yell out their names – annoyed that we were calling them back so soon. It had hardly been five minutes.

"Help me!" Yelena called again, looking up at us with indignation.

"We're going to wait for the jinn," Julian replied.

"I want to get out now! This place smells *weird*."

Despite Yelena's grumblings, we ended up waiting until the jinn arrived—she clearly wasn't badly hurt.

"What's going on?" Aisha asked, appearing suddenly and peering past us into the pit.

"Yelena fell into a pit," I replied.

Julian stifled a laugh, and Aisha glared at him.

"You tease that girl too much. Why didn't you get her out?" the jinni snapped.

"We were waiting for you!" I exclaimed.

Aisha tutted loudly, and in the next moment she had vanished, leaving us standing with a frowning Horatio.

A second later, Yelena was back up at the top, covered in dirt and looking furious.

"Thanks for your *help*," she said, with as much sarcasm as she could muster.

"Horatio"—Aisha ignored us all and looked to her husband—"come back down with me. There's a path leading from the bottom of the crater… I think we should look into it."

I turned to the jinni in surprise, but before I could comment, she and Horatio had vanished. I looked over the side of the pit and saw them floating toward the same edge we were on—the path must be leading beneath us.

"Come on," I said to the others, drawing them around to the other side of the pit so we could get a better view.

I moved as quickly as I could, my feet sliding on the softer mud of the edges, smacking down the brambles with my boots.

Just as we reached the opposite side, I heard voices echoing from the path they'd just followed. It was small—narrow enough that a single person could get through, but low...I doubted sentries could pass without some difficulty.

"Horatio, Aisha?" I called down.

The voices continued, but I couldn't make out what they were saying.

"Do you think we should go down?" Julian asked, already testing that the slope would hold us without creating a landslide.

"Uhh...Okay." Had they found the jinn? It was certainly a good hiding place—there was no way they would have been found unless they wanted to be. The path looked as if it had been created naturally. Had anyone other than the jinni come down here, they would have dismissed it as a natural formation caused by the crater.

We started climbing down—with difficulty. The soil was soft, but it kept crumbling away beneath us, and we ended up sliding most of the way.

"I'm glad I got out of this place just to go right back in," Yelena grumbled. She kept wincing when she put pressure on her ankle, and I was starting to worry that she was genuinely hurt.

"We should splint that ankle," I commented, glancing at her shoe.

"I've got bandages in my pack," Julian added. "I'll fix it when we get down."

But as we reached the bottom of the pit, Horatio and Aisha came into view. Looming behind them in a dark red robe was a familiar face.

"Zerus?"

What's he doing here?

My eyes widened as I came face-to-face with my kidnapper.

I hadn't seen him again after the night of the imperial trials, where he'd let the nymphs take him under their spell—I'd been left to wander the labyrinth in a daze, trying pointlessly to find a way out. I hadn't thought about him much after that, to be perfectly honest. I'd assumed he'd closeted himself away in Hellswan castle somewhere, keeping out of the way of his competitive brothers—I'd never really got the impression he was as desperate to win as Jenus or Tejus.

"Human boy," he replied, his expression indicating that he recognized me, but only vaguely.

"He's been living down here for a while," Aisha said.

I looked more closely at Zerus. He certainly seemed to be a bit out of it—not really all there. His eyes kept darting about the place like a trapped rabbit's, as if he might scuttle away at any moment.

"Did you come here to get away from the Acolytes?" I asked.

He looked at me with confusion, and shook his head.

"The entity?" I pressed.

"There's dark work at hand here, dark work," he muttered, his eyes shifting from mine to stare at the floor. He started to rock slowly, shifting from one foot to the other.

Aisha motioned us all to move away.

"He's obviously not well—mentally," she hissed. "I can't get a straight answer out of him. Is he Tejus's brother? He keeps mentioning that he's a Hellswan and that his brother's calling to him for help."

"Do you think it might be a trick?" I asked. "Why would Tejus call to him? And how? Can they communicate mentally at this distance—could Tejus reach him here?"

The jinni shrugged, but her eyes softened when she looked back at him.

"I'm not sure this is a trick. He certainly didn't want to be found—he didn't want Horatio or me anywhere near him."

"All right." I sighed. It wasn't like he could do much damage that hadn't been done already—we'd get him back to Tejus for him to deal with. "Let's question him on the jinn first, though. He might have seen something," I said, making my way back to Zerus's trembling figure.

"The end of Nevertide is coming," Zerus whispered to me as I approached, his voice raspy with fear. "My brother calls for me—he calls for me to save him."

His dark hair, worn long like Tejus's, was matted with leaves and mud. He was unshaven, but his cloak and the clothes beneath it were fairly clean. He'd obviously found a stream somewhere to wash himself—which indicated that he wasn't completely 'gone'.

"We'll get you to your brother soon," I replied in what I hoped was a soothing tone.

He looked even more horrified at that statement, so I changed the subject.

"We're looking for some jinn—creatures like those two." I pointed to Horatio and Aisha. "Have you seen anyone resembling them?"

Zerus looked at the jinn inquisitively, as if he was observing their strangeness for the first time.

"I haven't seen creatures like that." He shook his head in wonderment. "What did you call them, jinn?"

I nodded.

"I haven't seen their kind. But this forest is full of strange things…dark powers, whispers. Lights that flash from above, as if they are stars"—he looked up to the mountain range—"and shadows that creep in from the waters. Nevertide is no longer a safe place."

"What lights?" I asked.

"From the mountains. They come at night—there is power up there." He shivered and turned away.

"We need to get up to the mountain. Can you show us where

you saw the lights?" I asked.

"No! You shouldn't go up there, human—you should have left this place long ago when Tejus permitted you to leave. Why did you stay?"

I wanted to laugh. Clearly Zerus had been here a while—he'd missed out on a *lot*. I didn't think now was the right time to fill him in. "We can offer you help, Zerus. But we need to get to the mountain first—we're looking for a way to save Nevertide. We believe there are creatures up there that can stop this, stop the entity and the shadow. Please, help us?"

The sentry looked over at our group—two jinn and the three kids who professed they could save his land. He looked doubtful.

"I can lead you to the base of the mountain," he replied eventually, "and point you in the right direction of the lights, but then you must continue on your own." He looked despondent for a moment, observing the walls of the pit and the trees that surrounded us.

"I feel there is not much hope for you, little human… Not much hope at all."

SHERUS

I walked slowly to the window, looking for the stars in the rips of the sky. The rest of the land was bathed in a grotesque shade of yellow, as if the sun itself was sick and dying.

Another omen had awoken me—dark and as chilling as the rest, but, as always, with no tangible information that would be of any use to us. My gaze fixed on a single star that blazed through the rip. This single star burned more brightly than the rest. I fancied that it offered hope, a guiding light that told me the rest of the universe was safe—that at least the stars continued to shine, their skies intact, worlds turning as they should.

I wanted to speak to Derek again about the closing of the portal. I knew what I asked was a lot. I had placed a heavy burden on the Novak ruler. If we closed the portal, and could find no way out, then we would most likely perish at the hands of the entity and his army. Was the desolation of GASP too high a price to pay for the safety of the rest of the supernatural realm, Earth and the In-Between?

In my heart of hearts, I thought that it was not.

But then what? What if there came another threat in their absence? Would this decision save the creatures of the dimensions, only to have them perish later?

I turned away from the window. My maudlin fancies, I knew, could drive me close to madness.

Dressing quickly, I left the room, shutting my door behind me. Most of the palace was still active—I could hear the guards and ministers giving orders, and the raucous cries of the human children as they played some game.

Are you willing to lock innocents in here too, Sherus?

I strode with purpose down the corridor toward the main staircase. At the top, I met the jinni queen ascending. I faltered.

"Queen Nuriya." I bowed respectfully.

"King of the fire fae." She nodded back, her golden eyes dancing in the dim light of the palace. They reminded me of home—her irises were the very color of the fire opals that decorated my bedchamber.

"You look pale," she observed. "Has something happened?"

"No more than a dream." I smiled ruefully.

She frowned, her radiant skin lightly creasing at her forehead. "But these dreams of yours, were they not the very thing that alerted us to the dangers of the entity in the first place? Derek should be informed—it may indicate a shift in the entity's plans."

"I am on my way to inform him now," I assured her, surprised at how pleased I was to hear that she took my omens seriously—that she didn't believe they were the result of a dark and brooding mind as my sister did.

"I will accompany you," she replied. "Derek is wise, but vampires do not fully comprehend the subtleties of our magic—that the subconscious and the stars often hold more answers than mysteries."

I nodded in agreement, wholeheartedly delighting in the sentiment, but also distracted by the jet-black thickness of her hair and how it cast deep shadows against her face.

"Shall we be on our way?" she prompted.

"Uh, yes."

I continued my journey down the staircase and the queen glided beside me.

When we reached Derek, he was already in deep conversation with his granddaughter Hazel and the sentry commander. Tejus was a man who I had believed shared my stoic nature—who might be on my side when it came to shutting the portal...but his love for the Novak girl knew no bounds. If I suggested anything that might put her life in danger, along with the rest of them, I imagined he'd rather feed me to the entity himself.

"Sherus, Nuriya, just in time." Derek turned to us both. From his expression, I realized he'd just heard bad news. Tejus and Hazel both looked perturbed—the jinni queen was right. Something had changed.

Derek told me about the visions of the sentry—the shadow seeping out to Earth's dimensions, and by the sounds of Hazel's description, the In-Between itself.

"Then I implore you, Derek. Let us find a way to close the portal—before the rest of the dimensions fall to the hands of this creature. I too had an interrupted sleep; visions not as clear as Tejus's, but I believe they are true premonitions of what is to come if we do not halt his destruction. I heard the stars of the fae screaming, portals ripping, and my kin blackened by the shadow... I fear we are *all* doomed, Derek, if the entity is released from this cage."

The vampire studied me with intelligent eyes, but I could see his focus was miles away, strategizing how best to accomplish this task without putting his family and friends in danger.

"We will." He nodded. "Let me assemble a team to watch the cove. We have to wait for the right moment, or we won't have a chance. The portal is too carefully watched—clearly the entity suspects what we might try to do. What bothers me is that Tejus's vision was so clear...does it know we will try to stop it, believing that we can't? Or is it something else altogether? A trick to distract us?"

"From what?" I asked. "There is no greater crime than the one shown to Tejus. I believe the entity is taunting us, so confident that it cannot fail it is willing for its plans to be seen—and it will laugh at our efforts to try to stop it."

"Perhaps," Derek mused.

"I think Sherus is right," Tejus muttered. "I think we have no further options than to close the portal…but I want some of us out before we do."

He looked at Hazel, his gaze determined.

As I suspected, the sentry would happily sacrifice his life for hers. I wondered for a moment if my heart would ever feel that way again, or if I was too old and jaded—had seen too much to experience the violent and altering emotions of love.

Park your melancholy, Sherus! I scolded myself.

We were attempting to save the dimensions from annihilation, and yet here I was like an old and weepy king, mourning some abstract emotion.

"Let us make plans then," Queen Nuriya replied, bringing me back to the present. "Let us find a way to lock the entity in."

TEJUS

"Commander, excuse the intrusion—two of the flying creatures request your attention."

A guard stood to attention at the door of the banquet hall, his eyes searching me out from the rest of those assembled at the table. I rose, wondering which creature he could mean—one of the dragons or the Hawks?

"Let me come," Hazel murmured, "they might have news from Benedict."

I nodded, and we both followed the guard out of the room. The debate was almost at an end anyway, Derek had made his decision as to who would join him on lookout at the cove, waiting for an opportunity that we might use to our advantage to shut the portal.

We crossed the lawns, over to the edge of the barrier where two of the Hawk boys stood waiting for us. They carried huge bouquets of flowers in their arms, and I stared at them in confusion.

"Is this some strange custom I'm not familiar with?" I murmured to Hazel.

She shook her head. "No...I have no idea what they're doing."

We quickened our pace. When we reached them, the Hawk boys were grinning broadly.

"You've got to take these off our hands," one of them said, a boy with bright aquamarine eyes. "I feel like I've just had about twenty coffees—I'm getting a headache."

"From the flowers?" Hazel asked doubtfully.

"Try them." He proffered the bunch into Hazel's arms. She grabbed them, looking sidelong at me with a bemused expression.

"Oh, wow," she gasped, her eyes wide.

"What is it?" I pressed.

"They're filled with energy—crazy powerful energy," the boy with green-blue eyes replied.

"He's right." Hazel turned to me, placing the flowers gently on the ground and keeping only one. They glowed brightly, their center a deep pink hue that pulsed like the heart of a flame.

"Try it." She offered a flower to me and I took it. I felt the energy instantly—it coursed through my veins, its power comparable with the stones that had locked in the entity and his army.

"Are we sure these are safe? Where did you find them?" I asked the Hawk boys.

"We found them in the forest—an entire field of them, in the middle of nowhere. The jinn checked them for magic. They said the flowers seemed natural—there was no evidence that they'd been tampered with."

Their reassurance mollified me somewhat, but I was still skeptical. Everything about them seemed so similar to the stones—the colors were the same unnatural hue, the power felt the same...

"How have these never been discovered before?" Hazel asked. "Did you know about them?"

I shook my head. "No, but if they were found in the depths of the forest then that doesn't surprise me. Few venture in there...though you say they were in a meadow? I've flown near the Dauoa many times—surely I would have seen the lights?"

The Hawk boys shrugged. Clearly no one had any answers. I had to weigh up the potential danger of these plants against the undoubted benefits they would bring to the entire army—all of us were in need of the energy they could provide.

I quickly made my choice.

"Guards." I addressed the sentries who were nearby, watching us with unabashed curiosity and delight. "Deliver these to those in need—the ministers who are upholding the barriers especially."

The guards hastened to their duty.

Once the flowers were all gone, aside from two that Hazel and I held, the Hawks turned to me, concern taking over from the initial delight they'd felt at delivering such a gift.

"We hoped that the battle would be won—but it's not, is it?" one of them asked.

"The entity holds too much power," I replied. "We have one option now, which is to lock the portal. There's no other way out of Nevertide. The entity plans to seep out into the rest of the dimensions—this is the only way to stop it. I'm afraid that our survival might rest on you finding the jinn. The witches are positive now that the creatures still reside here…somewhere."

"We'll find them," the first Hawk replied, his aquamarine eyes flashing with conviction. "We won't stop until we do."

* * *

When the Hawks left, Hazel and I made our way back to the palace.

My mind kept returning to the vision I'd had. How it had felt, rather than what I'd seen. Almost as if the entity had been there with me somehow—delving into my mind, planting the visions itself. If that were true, it would mean that the entity had managed to find a way to mind-meld with me. How that was possible at such a distance, I couldn't fathom, but I couldn't shake the feeling that my suspicions were correct. If it *were* true, that left me with another puzzle. I had felt a similar sensation when Hazel and I had created that barrier, but I couldn't put that down to the entity…Why would it help us discover a way to defend ourselves? To get away just at the point when it could have killed us?

"Before I leave for the cove we should practice creating the barrier again," I said to Hazel, thinking that I might be able to understand better if I could feel it again—my theories might be completely misguided. Now that we had the added energy of the flowers, there was no need to worry about draining myself before we left for the mission.

"I don't want you to go to the cove," Hazel whispered. "I know it's important, but I have a bad feeling about all of this. I don't know what it is…I just don't know if this is the best plan."

"It might not be," I admitted, "but it's the only one we have. We can't wait for the jinn to be found—it's too risky. Even if they are discovered, they might be unwilling or unable to help."

Hazel nodded, sighing. We were about to walk up to the front steps, but I pulled her back. We didn't need to be at the meeting. I trusted her instincts—if this mission was ill-advised, then I wanted to spend the last moments I had with her.

"Hazel," I began, not truly knowing what it was that I wanted to say. I wanted to offer some reassurance, but what good would that do? She knew the slim chance of success that we were facing—she wouldn't be fooled by false hope. Perhaps, as always with Hazel, honesty was the best policy.

"I should have married you," I blurted out. Hazel's eyes widened, taken aback as I drew her into my arms. "As soon as I could. Not involved myself with the trials, left it all to Ash sooner. That will be my only regret—that I didn't—"

"*Stop*," she urged. "We're going to have time for all of that later. We will, Tejus, I have to keep believing that."

She drew her arms around me, pulling me into a kiss. It left me breathless and aching.

"I don't want you to go to the cove thinking this is a suicide mission. It *won't* be—forget what I said. Please. You have to come back to me. Ash survived, against all the odds, and you will too. We're all going to get out of here. We're going to live our lives out in The Shade, with a family—children, and grandchildren, great-grandchildren—surrounded by friends and family. We're going to die of old age, many, many years from now, or we're going to live for eternity—whatever we choose. But it will be *our* choice, not the entity's. It doesn't get to decide our future. It can ruin this land, it can try to ruin others, but it won't destroy what we have."

I held her head cradled in my hands, gently brushing the tears that had fallen onto her cheeks.

"Okay," I promised her, "I'll come back to you. I promise."

I held her tightly against my chest. She hugged me fiercely, her arms wrapped around my waist. I looked out in the direction of the cove. I couldn't see the shadow I knew would be hovering above the portal, but I vowed that what I'd just promised Hazel would be the truth—I would return to her.

Whatever happened, I would return.

Ben

My father had decided that Sherus, Tejus, Aiden, Lucas and I would join him on the mission to the cove. We would be accompanied by Lethe, the ice dragon, and Nuriya and Ibrahim to close the portal if we got a chance.

I said my goodbyes to River and Grace, wishing that I could one day put a stop to the pain I brought River in these moments. Of course, she understood GASP's role and continually put her own life on the line, but it was never easy for her… I guessed that came from me dying once already.

The ministers created a rip in the barrier for us to pass, and we left the palace behind, the crowds of sentries and GASP members standing silently behind us.

"I don't want to transport us straight to the cove... We don't know what will meet us when we get there. I think it would be prudent to use a cloaking spell instead. I don't know if the entity or its army will be able to see through it, but it's worth trying," Ibrahim informed us as we reached the start of the path.

"Good idea," my father replied. "Lethe?" He turned to the dragon.

"I'll rely on my own stealth to remain unseen," Lethe replied.

A moment later, Ibrahim's spell was upon everyone but Lethe. The ice dragon was under strict instruction not to fly until we were sure that the entity was distracted. If its armies saw us now, we would be done for. It would make our journey to the cove longer, but that was fine—it was better to be cautious.

When we got partway down the track, my dad motioned to the outskirts of the forest on either side.

"We should keep to the trees, just in case they can see through Ibrahim's spell. I think we'll be okay, as long as we don't venture into the forest."

We all stepped into their shade. The sun was starting to set and it made the shadows of the trees long and dense. This light would make it easier for the armies to creep up on us without our noticing. I just hoped the feeling of dread that usually accompanied them would be enough of a warning.

"Can you see anything yet?" I asked Tejus as we drew closer to the cove.

He nodded, squinting in the direction of the water. "It seems unchanged—the shadow looms over the portal. I can't see any sign of Jenus though. We might have to get closer before I can tell."

I nodded, relieved that the armies hadn't yet left through the portal.

"What's it waiting for?" Sherus hissed.

"Perhaps more of its kind?" I suggested. "The planet in the In-Between is full of the stones. They might have broken open at the same time these did—the beings they imprisoned could be making their way here through the portal?"

The fae king looked at me in horror.

"Then we are already too late!" he exclaimed in a whisper.

My father turned around and shook his head.

"Not necessarily. If Tejus's visions are correct, then the entity is organizing a well-strategized attack. Ben's right—it might be trying to unify its forces here before deploying them."

"You're saying they won't wreak havoc on Earth and the In-Between as they make their way here?" Sherus replied skeptically.

"I'm saying that they *might* not," my father emphasized.

The fae king sighed, his face dark with anger. Queen Nuriya placed a small hand on his arm, and to my surprise, he visibly calmed.

We moved closer, the only sound our footsteps on the dried

leaves and bracken and the faint sounds of our breathing mingling with the increasingly chilled air.

Eventually we reached the small path that led down to the cove.

"Do you have a clear view?" my dad asked Tejus.

"Yes, I can see Jenus," the sentry muttered. "He's standing by the shore...It looks like he's waiting for something. He's pacing up and down."

My father looked around. We were well sheltered by the trees here, but if we moved further ahead we would be at the edge of the cliff, sheltered by some large rocks that had been thrown up by a tear in the earth.

"We move ahead," my dad announced, pointing at the cliff edge, "and we wait there for our moment."

To get to the rock we would have to cross a clear path, one that was in direct view of the shadow that hovered over the portal entrance.

"Ibrahim, can you transport us to the rocks?" Derek asked the warlock.

He nodded, and a moment later, we were standing right by the rocks—Nuriya appearing at Sherus's side a second later by her own magic. Now it was only Lethe left on the other side.

I held my breath as he scurried across the path. It wasn't wide, but for those few moments he was completely exposed. I could hear Lethe's heart pounding as he collapsed next to me.

We all waited to see if they'd spotted us. I dared to look over the rock, seeing if there was any movement from the shadow or Jenus, but all remained the same. I heaved a sigh of relief. Ibrahim's cloaking spell was still over us.

"What now, do we just wait?" Aiden asked. "There must be another way—what if they don't move?"

"We have to hope that they will," my dad replied. "It's too dangerous to venture down there now."

We all sat and watched. The sun dipped lower on the horizon, the sky becoming almost beautiful with its pink and purple hues. Now we were close to the shadow, I could feel the foreboding sense of dread and discomfort that its presence had brought about before. My stomach churned at the unnaturalness of it—the evil that it suggested, as if the shadow only knew how to destroy, as if it existed as the exact opposite of everything that was good in the world.

"Keep your eyes on the stars, Benjamin," Sherus murmured at me.

I did as he asked. I focused on the cold, bright pinpricks in the velvet of the night, and soon the presence of the shadow started to bother me less.

I was being lulled into a false sense of security.

A moment later, I heard a loud screeching—screams of triumph, echoing from the portal. I jumped, my heart rate accelerating. Storming through the portal were hordes of ghouls—their graying skin stretched over skulls with sparse patches of hair hanging off them, their clawed fingers outstretched, their mouths open, sharp teeth and black tongues lusting for flesh.

Ghouls?

What were they doing here? It was the last thing we'd expected to see. Where had they even come from? The ghouls swarmed around the cove, disordered and screeching, so many that their forms started blocking the land below, whizzing around the cliff face. Soon they were traveling so high up the cliff-face that they were only a few feet below us. If even one of them smelt us, or sensed our presence in any way, we would be done for.

I didn't dare open my mouth, but knew that the others would be thinking the same thing.

The ground started to rumble—slight tremors that rattled the stones and dirt by my feet. I looked at the shadow, but it hadn't moved from its position...what was causing the earth to shake?

My eyes were drawn to the portal. We heard a loud gurgling noise, like a plug being pulled, and then the blood drained from my face. A loud wailing noise emanated from the mouth of the portal—heavy, wet cries that came from some wretched creature...I knew that sound. It was one I had hoped to never hear again.

The ghoul queen.

Sherus gripped my forearm. The fae king recognized it too.

The portal yawned open, and the ghoul queen emerged. She heaved her paunchy rolls of fat forward, their glutinous appearance making me sick to my stomach. Her cold blue veins were stretched beneath her translucent skin like marble, and she wore the grotesque crown that I'd seen her in last—an assortment of black and green decaying teeth proudly adorning her head. The lank strands of hair trembled with the effort of moving her ginormous figure.

"Ben?" my dad hissed at me as quietly as he could. "Do you know this creature?"

I nodded, trying to find my voice.

"She was in The Underworld—the residence of the ghouls," I added for the benefit of the others, "I was trapped there in ghost form. I saw her deep underground. The Necropolis, it was called—the furthest depths of The Underworld. I saw her moving through a graveyard of ghosts, wailing like she is now. We left her…Aisha tried to kill her, but she vanished. I didn't think she would ever emerge." *I didn't think I would ever see her again.* The fae and ghouls had engaged in a battle soon after Sherus granted me my fae body—I was aware that not all the Underworld ghouls had been wiped out, but I'd thought the queen would have been one of them.

Some stones are better left unturned…

That was the exact thought I'd had after we'd left that queen alive in The Underworld's depths… I couldn't help but wonder now if she was a stone we *should* have unturned while we'd had the chance.

"Do you know why she might be here?" my father asked.

I shook my head. I had no idea why she would be appearing in Nevertide…Unless, of course, the entity was drawing all the dark supernatural creatures here to join its forces? It seemed so unlikely. The ghouls were not known for building allegiances with other supernatural creatures. The only exception that I'd heard of was the deal with the fae—but that had been to serve their purposes only. What might the entity have offered them?

I kept watching, barely able to tear my eyes away from the repugnant queen. She certainly hadn't improved with age. She lumbered forward, and then Jenus stepped into view.

Instantly, the wailing stopped.

The queen's face transformed. The rolls of fat beneath her chin wobbled like jelly, her fleshy gray lips splitting open into…a *smile?*

Jenus's arms opened and she lumbered into his embrace. Her sharp black claws clutched at his soiled robe, her face bearing down toward his. The last rays of sun glared brilliantly in their final descent, and Jenus cried out in exultation before his lips, wetted in excitement by an anxious tongue, leapt onto hers. Their putrid bodies drew together as they grunted into a lustful kiss.

Bile burned at the back of my throat.

One of us dry-heaved—I thought it might have been Tejus, but I could not look away to check.

Suddenly, the screeching of the ghouls stopped. En masse, they darted down to the ground. Slithering like eels against one another, they all bowed down low before Jenus, and then turned, scraping the floor once again to honor the shadow.

What is going on?

My mind searched frantically for understanding. Clearly there was a hierarchy of evil here—the ghouls acknowledged that they were lesser beings than the entity and its shadow…and the entity had clearly just been reunited with a long-lost companion. Had it been what the ghoul queen had been wailing for, yearning for, all that time ago in The Underworld? Wandering the graveyards, waiting for its return? *Binge-eating ghosts to cope with her misery?*

I thought about what the Impartial Ministers, Tejus and Ash had told us about the entity. How whatever creatures were contained in those stones were the first inhabitants of Nevertide. Had the entity and its queen somehow been parted in the supernatural realm when it had been banished to the stone lock? Were the entity and the ghoul queen somehow of the same species?

My mind boggled. I looked across at my father and Sherus, both as stunned as me at the unfolding of events.

"What the *hell* is happening here?" Tejus breathed.

"I have no idea," I replied slowly, "but this has to be the most traumatizing thing I've ever witnessed."

Tejus grimaced.

Clearly I wasn't alone.

ASH

When Tejus and the other members of GASP left for the cove, I went in search of the Impartial Ministers. I still had unanswered questions about the water, and more specifically, the effect on my mortal life.

I found them sitting in an empty room in the palace, nursing a flagon of mead. They had clearly been drinking for some time—the air was thick with its heady, sweet scent. I observed them with disgust. The guards and ministers of Nevertide were out in the grounds, doing what they could to protect the land and its people. Not to mention members of GASP, and Tejus, risking their lives down at the cove. If the Impartial Ministers were meant to represent a 'brotherhood' of Nevertide, then they were doing a horrendous job of it.

Their glazed eyes slowly turned in my direction, and they both frowned at the intrusion.

"Emperor of Nevertide," one of them slurred. "We are celebrating the end—will you bother someone else? This is a ritual. All beasts must mourn what is lost, and sentries are no different."

"Ritual?" I spat. "I only see two broken fools, drinking like cowards."

"How dare you?" the second blustered. "We have given our very souls to this land—we have watched it thrive for centuries, and now it is our burden to watch it fall."

I tried to keep my temper in check. There was absolutely no point in trying to tell them that Nevertide had never 'thrived' under their watch, and that it wasn't the end—not yet. Not while we had men and women still willing to fight for it.

"I was healed by the immortal waters," I began impatiently. "I was close to death, wounded by the shadow. But it healed me—completely, not even a scar. When I emerged, I was told by three of your kind that I was now part of the brotherhood, that I was immortal...I want to know, is this true?"

That got their attention.

Both of them were looking at me with varying degrees of shock and fury.

"Those waters are sacred—not for the likes of *you*!"

I rolled my eyes.

"What does it mean?" I asked again, the palm of my hand resting against the pommel of my new sword. If I had to threaten them to get the answers I needed, I happily would.

"It means you are one of us," muttered one of them. "Now the immortal waters have blessed you, you have obtained a degree of immortality, and will live many lifetimes after this one."

"What does that mean exactly? Alive till the end of time? Impervious to weapons?" I asked, sick to death of their vague answers.

"We are not impervious to weapons," the first minister sighed, as if my questions were some great philosophical debate that was wearing him down, "though we can be healed time and time again by the waters. And no, it does not mean to the end of time—eventually you *will* die, unless you preserve yourself within the waters."

"And I will age?" I questioned, though the answer was right in front of me.

"You will age."

And Ruby won't.

"How old are you?" I asked.

The Impartial Ministers looked at one another and laughed, hacking and wheezing.

"We have lived for nine hundred years," one replied. "Almost a millennium."

I nodded, speechless.

That's old.

"But I'm not in any way now tied to Nevertide—I mean, I don't have to remain here to stay alive?"

Since the first conversation with the ministers it had weighed on my mind, that somehow my life might be inextricably linked to the land.

The one minister who had answered my questions eyed me with curiosity.

"No. You're not physically linked with this land, Ashbik. Though, I must say, it is a curious question for one who seems so determined to save it...I wonder if that answer pleases or displeases you?"

For once the Impartial Ministers had hit the nail on the head. The sentry's insight was surprising, and for a moment I didn't know how to answer him—or if I should even bother.

"I don't want my life to be linked to Nevertide," I replied slowly, wondering, even as the words left my mouth, how true that statement was.

The minister picked up his cup once again, and drained the liquid with a hearty gulp.

"You may find," he continued, wiping away droplets of the vile liquid that spilled onto his beard, "that though you are not physically linked to this land, your heart and soul may have something different to say on the matter."

"Perhaps," I murmured, not wishing to discuss the issue any further. I knew where my heart was linked—and it was to Ruby, and that was all.

"I'll leave you to stew in your misery," I replied, moving back toward the door. The Impartial Ministers both raised their cups once more, and went back to muttering between themselves.

I shut the door behind me, relieved to be away from them.

Walking back outside to the palace grounds, I tried to ignore what the ministers had said about being linked to Nevertide. There was no use dwelling on it anyway—there might not *be* a Nevertide by tomorrow, not unless we found a way to halt the entity. Or, if the team found a way for the portal to be locked, we'd be stuck here, fighting the entity's army till we no longer could.

As I stepped outside, I shivered in the cold air.

The evening was silent. The sentries guarding the borders were tense and anxious, murmuring quietly to one another or not at all. The guards stood watch silently, their gaze never leaving the sky for more than a few moments.

"Ash?"

Ruby approached from the other side of the terrace, wrapped up in a robe over her GASP uniform.

"Hey, Shortie." I smiled.

"I've been looking for you—do you think they're okay?" She

came to stand next to me, looking out in the direction of the cove. "I'm glad you didn't go."

"I hope so," I replied.

I didn't know how I felt about being left behind. I knew and understood Derek's reasoning—that if the mission were to fail, then the sentries would need a leader. Along with the rest of GASP, we would need to be the last defense against the entity and its army.

"I'm worried about Tejus—and Hazel. What she'd do if anything happened to him. I've been there, and I wouldn't wish it on my worst enemy." She leaned her head against my chest, her hand idly grazing against my arm as if to check that I was still all there. She'd done this a few times since I'd come out of the immortal waters and I didn't think she even realized that she was doing it.

"I'm here," I replied softly. "You don't have to worry. I'm not going anywhere."

She nodded, not replying. I guessed the sentiment wasn't entirely true—we didn't know what would happen tonight. Whether or not we would survive to see the dawn.

"Ruby, I wanted to thank you for saving my life. It must have been difficult, riding with me all that way, not knowing. It was amazing. *You're* amazing."

She smiled, poking me in the ribs. "You don't have to say thank you. Just stay alive, okay?"

"Will do," I murmured.

I wanted to talk to her about Claudia's offer, if she would want me to seriously consider it at some point—especially considering the differences our aging process would result in if she were to become a vampire and I didn't.

Before I could open my mouth to say anything, the ground started to tremble. Ruby's grip on me tightened, and we looked down at the stone beneath our feet. The mortar started to crack slightly, the surface shuddering just enough to dislodge some of the paving.

"Is it coming?" Ruby whispered.

"I don't know."

I rushed out onto the yard, Ruby following behind me. The ministers and guards were looking around, waiting for my instruction. Members of GASP flooded out from the palace doors, ready to help. Claudia and Yuri rushed up to us, Claudia instantly taking her daughter's hand.

"What do we do?" one of the witches asked, her voice hoarse with fear.

"Secure the borders!" I yelled to everyone, waving GASP over to the ministers to provide the necessary energy.

I glanced up at the sky.

I couldn't see or feel anything yet—but it didn't mean that it wasn't coming.

TEJUS

A procession started to form. Jenus and the monstrous crowned female ghoul began leading the rest of the creatures in the direction of the forest that bordered the opposite side of the cove.

I waited anxiously for Jenus and his queen to disappear from view. I could feel the others growing restless beside me, all of us hoping that this would be our chance. If the procession left the portal unguarded, then we'd have enough time to lock it, or perhaps even better, if we were sure we'd get enough time, we could ensure the villagers, Hazel and the others got to safety first.

"Where are they headed?" Derek asked.

The forest they were walking into bordered Hellswan castle,

eventually leading up to its front gates. Beyond the castle lay the summer palace and further in the distance, the mountain range, all surrounded by more forest.

"I think they're headed toward Hellswan—there's not much else that lies in that direction."

We continued to watch the cove. Once the last ghouls left, part of the shadow remained hovering over the portal. I gritted my teeth in irritation—had they left the ghouls guarding it, we would have had a much easier job. Clearly the entity was well aware that the portal was its one way out of Nevertide—it wouldn't leave it open to our interference.

"What now?" Lucas asked, his face ghostly pale.

"We split up," Derek replied. "Sherus, Nuriya, Ibrahim, wait by the portal to see if anything changes. If you can get closer without the shadow detecting you, do—but don't take any risks."

All of them nodded, the jinni queen's gaze darting across the landscape of the cove, already plotting where she might reappear without being seen.

"The rest of us are going to follow Jenus and the rest of them to the castle. Do we need to follow them through the forest, or is there another way?" Derek asked me.

"We can follow the path—it will lead to the castle, probably faster than they can reach it," I mused, "which makes me wonder why they chose that route in the first place."

Ben's eyebrows rose inquisitively.

"Perhaps they're in no hurry. Clearly the shadow feels more comfortable among the trees, and ghouls like the damp."

A moment later I heard a ferocious howl coming from the forest. It was followed by the loud snapping of bones and ghouls' laughter. *Ah.*

"They're feeding," I muttered. "That makes sense."

That part of the forest was overrun with fang beasts, no doubt providing intestines for the ghouls' evening meal. More howls went up, and the wild shrieks of ghouls enjoying the hunt.

"Let's go," Derek commanded. "Ibrahim, can you provide us with cover?"

The warlock nodded, casting us under his spell. The dragon, Lethe, refused – preferring to fly up and out of sight.

The shadow didn't move as we made our way along the path. I had half hoped that it would, giving the warlock and jinni enough time to close the portal undisturbed.

"How far to Hellswan?" Ben asked me.

"A few miles, nothing more—we should be there soon."

We kept the pace steady as we continued on the road through Nevertide. If the vampires were irritated by having to move at a slower pace than they were used to, they didn't show it.

As we drew closer to our destination, the sounds of the ghouls cavorting grew louder. Their evident joy at taking over the land was sickening—was this what it had been like when the entity

A TIDE OF WAR

had ruled here? Had all of Nevertide's more twisted creatures been free to prowl and hunt in this way? It made me wonder why human settlers had ever wanted to stay within its shores. Perhaps they had been of the same mind as the Acolytes, falsely believing the entity to be benevolent and an all-powerful god, before it was too late.

"We should veer off path here—edge around the side of the castle, otherwise we'll end up arriving at the portcullis at the same time they do," I murmured. Even if the ghouls couldn't see us, the chance that the entity might be able to *sense* us made a direct arrival too risky.

"Stay vigilant," Derek reminded us, "they might have sent lookouts on ahead."

I led the group off the path as soon as we came to the start of the ruined village. We moved silently between two burnt-out homes, up into the farmland behind them. Once we reached the edge of the property, we were back in the forest again, making our way through the densely packed trees and viciously spiked undergrowth.

We exited the forest where the far eastern tower once stood. Here the ground sloped upward, and at the top, the remains of the castle's outer wall lay in crumbled ruins. Lethe joined us, and we watched in silence – waiting for the ghoul hordes to arrive.

We didn't have long to wait.

As soon as we were in position, we saw the procession making its way through the forest. The ghouls had lit branches to make flaming torches, and they held these aloft, chanting guttural noises as they approached the castle.

Jenus and the ghoul queen had been given cloaks made from dead fang beast fur, blood still running off the skin and dripping down onto the bodies of the wearers. It was repulsive—my heart quickened in anger on watching such repugnant creatures striding through the portcullis, desecrating the land where my home had once stood.

"Peace, Tejus," Lethe whispered next to me. I guessed he was afraid I might rush forward and try to slaughter them. "You'll get your revenge—we just need to be patient."

I nodded, unable to speak.

Once Jenus and the queen entered the grounds, the ghouls and the shadow dispersed, flying off around the rubble of the castle, upturning the stones and dragging the rotting corpses of sentries up from their resting places.

Zerus could be one of those.

I hadn't seen him when we'd come to find the emperor's book, but that didn't mean he wasn't here somewhere— disfigured beyond recognition or buried too far down for me to see him.

We ducked down further as the ghouls approached. Fortunately for us, they didn't seem to be aware that they might be being watched, having too much fun in their mockery of the dead to pay close attention to their surroundings.

"What do you think they're doing here?" Ben asked, his voice barely even a whisper.

I had been wondering the same thing.

"I suppose that in a way, Hellswan castle is the home of the entity—if it was locked here for so many lifetimes, perhaps it wishes to return to it, to claim it as its own."

Ben looked skeptical. "If I was a prisoner somewhere for so long, I doubt I would ever want to return."

The intensity of the ghouls' cries picked up. The shadow, previously spreading out across where the entrance of the castle had once been, now moved backward, rejoining Jenus and the queen who stood by the outer wall.

"Something's happening," I said, shifting in my crouched position.

The earth began to tremble once more—this time it felt like it was coming from deep beneath the ground. Was Jenus calling on another supernatural beast to join him? The rubble of the castle started to shake. Any walls still left standing were sent crashing to the ground. An ear-splitting crack tore across the land where the castle stood.

Sending chunks of the gray stone flying backward, dark shapes emerged from the ground. We lowered ourselves further down behind the wall, avoiding the shards of splintering rock that hurtled our way.

I watched in utter disbelief as a gigantic hulk of black, slippery stone emerged from beneath Hellswan. Spiked turrets rose into the air and windowless towers of incredible scale bore down from above us. It was like a giant, forgotten creature pushing its way above the earth—buried for so many years, but completely untouched by the passing of time. The fortress gave the impression of being entirely carved from one piece of rock—I could see absolutely no evidence of joints, stonework or man's labor. It was as if the depths of Nevertide had created this monstrosity itself.

"This must have been the entity's home before it was banished to the lock," Ben whispered in awe.

The fortress must have remained buried for centuries. A cold chill moved down my spine as I imagined it miles beneath where I'd slept—its silent, monolithic structure waiting to be unearthed.

We watched as the ghouls swept in through a large black arch at its center, disappearing into the belly of the fortress. Their cries became hollow echoes, oppressed by the sheer size of the rock.

"Enough," Derek breathed. "We should get back to the portal. See how the others are doing. Lucas, head to the palace, let the rest of GASP and the army know what's happened here."

Gladly, I turned away from the sight of the fortress. Derek gestured that we should move back the way we had come. We moved as silently as we could back toward the trees.

Do you think that you can hide from me?

I froze. The voice of the entity whispered through the darkness, the soft tones brushing against my temples and worming its way inside of me. I spun around, seeing Jenus still miles away, walking slowly up to the fortress with his ghoul queen beside him.

I see everything, Tejus of Hellswan.

The others had stopped in their tracks too. Foolishly, I had hoped that now the entity had chosen a physical form, it would no longer be able to observe us in quite the same way—clearly I had been wrong.

I know you are watching me. But there's nothing you can do to stop me. Not now. Your powers are insignificant, your efforts wasted. You cannot conceive of what I have in store for you. Just know that my revenge will be swift, merciless and absolute... The end of days is nigh, my friends.

We looked at one another, too tired and beaten down to be surprised that the entity had known what we were doing all along.

"Let us leave," urged Derek again, his fangs protruding—the only indication of the rage that was simmering below the surface. "Ben, race ahead. Let Ibrahim and the others know that the entity is watching."

If they attempted to make a move toward the portal now, it

would be fatal.

As I dashed toward the trees, the last few words of the entity played on my mind. *You cannot conceive of what I have in store for you'*—was that true? Hadn't the entity shown me *exactly* what was to come? Or was this more evidence that I shouldn't believe the visions? That they were lies planted by the entity to distract us?

There was something I was missing here, I could feel it—something about the energy surge that had helped Hazel and me at the barrier, and then the feeling while I was receiving the visions that there was some alien, additional power present...

"Faster!" Derek called out.

Ignoring my thoughts, I ran, pushing my muscles till they screamed, mindlessly following the blurs of the vampires ahead.

Julian

I looked over at Zerus, his dark features lit up by the campfire.

We'd stopped for the night, finding a spot at the foothills of the mountain range where Aisha and Horatio had put up barriers, enabling us to remain unseen by any creatures that might wander by in search of a meal.

Zerus was strange. I didn't know if it was due to the weeks spent in isolation in the pit, or just because all the Hellswans were an odd bunch as far as I was concerned, but the guy didn't seem to be all *there*. At Benedict's insistence, he had agreed to guide us to a path that would lead up to the top of the mountain safely, but I felt that his strange mutterings and the slow, shuffling pace that he moved at would do nothing but delay us.

"Why don't we ask the Hawks to just fly us up?" I asked Benedict for what felt like the millionth time.

"What if we miss the jinn? If we're with the Hawks we're not going to be able to see properly," he replied reasonably.

I glanced over at Zerus to see if he was listening in to our conversation, but he seemed more preoccupied with his hunting knife, sharpening it with a stone. The scene didn't exactly make me feel comforted.

"Don't you think he's a bit of a liability, like he might snap at any moment?" I whispered.

Benedict contemplated the sentry for a few moments, and then shook his head.

"No. Not really—and what if he does? We've got Aisha, Horatio and Ridan here. They'll be able to calm him. I don't think he's out to harm us anyway, he's not like Jenus or anything."

I looked up to the tops of the trees, searching for Field, Fly and Sky. They hadn't been down for a while, not since Field and Fly had returned to us with news of the failed battle. It looked like all hope was resting on us bringing the jinn out of hiding, wherever they were, but we'd seen no evidence so far that the forest was populated by anything other than goblins and a loopy sentry.

"Get some rest, Julian," Benedict yawned at me. Yelena had already fallen asleep in front of the fire, hogging the best spot, of course.

"You get some sleep," I replied crossly. "I'll keep watch."

Aisha, Horatio and Ridan had already started to doze off, claiming that we were safe within their barriers, but I wasn't so sure. One thing I'd learned about Nevertide was that you couldn't be too careful—especially in the woods.

"Fine," he replied lazily, "you keep watch. Wake me up in a couple of hours and I'll take over."

He curled up in his GASP-issue sleeping bag and almost immediately started snoring.

'Wake me in a couple of hours?' Yeah right. Once Benedict was out, he was out. It would be like trying to wake the dead.

The firelight was dying out. It was just Zerus and me left awake, and it made me uncomfortable. Every so often I would catch the sentry studying me intently, then he'd go back to sharpening his blade—a repetitive scrape of stone against steel that was starting to irritate the heck out of me.

"Will you stop that?" I asked eventually.

"Does it bother you?" he asked, surprised.

"Yes, it bothers me," I replied, wondering if his dumbfounded expression was a trick or if he was genuinely a bit mad.

"I'm sorry, human creature," he replied awkwardly. "It's been a while since I was around anyone. Even back at the castle, I wasn't that keen on companionship—I like to keep to myself, though I realize it can make me...*off-putting* to others."

"It's fine," I grumbled, feeling a bit foolish.

He shrugged, putting the hunting knife away. He lay back, his hands crossed behind his head, staring up at the stars. A few moments later I heard the sounds of deep breathing. He too had fallen asleep.

* * *

The night was still. The Hawks didn't return, and I imagined that they'd found somewhere more suitable to rest, probably up in the branches of some tree. The fire was smoking gently, with only dying embers left glowing on the ground.

My job as lookout was slow going. Occasionally I heard a crack of twigs in the distance, but if there were animals about they didn't come any closer—either the barriers were doing their job, or we weren't particularly appealing to them. The lack of any real threat had an annoying consequence—I started to imagine shapes in the darkness. Rocks became hunched men, watching us from afar. Gnarled trees became strange creatures, their twigs claws, their unearthed roots long-reaching tentacles waiting to pull me into seas of dead leaves.

I shuddered, trying to maintain my grip on reality, but every time I managed to calm myself down, I would see another shape out of the corner of my eye—another lurking thing, waiting to grab me.

Calm down, idiot.

I settled back against a rock, and stared up at the sky. It was more calming this way. We were sheltered from winds down here, but at the top of the trees there was a slight breeze, parting the boughs so that every so often I could see the multitudes of stars shining across the sky—millions and millions of light years away.

"No, I can't help you, brother—no, please—*no.*"

Zerus was moaning in his sleep. He had been making small exhales of panicked breath on and off for a while now, but this was the first coherent thing I'd hear him utter. I watched him, waiting to hear more.

"I can't—I don't know how," he cried softly. Clearly whatever he was dreaming about was causing him a lot of anguish. Why did he think that Tejus needed his help so badly? Was he somehow communicating with him? Was the entity back at the palace? His moaning continued, and I wondered if I should wake him. For all I knew, the mind-meld bond was stronger in relatives—maybe he *was* conversing with Tejus.

I stood up. I wanted to know what he thought his brother needed him for so badly—if GASP and the other sentries were in danger, then I wanted to know about it.

"Zerus?" I shook him gently. "Wake up. You're having a bad dream."

The sentry opened his eyes, staring up at me. In the glow of the fire I could just make out the tears streaming down his cheeks.

"Human?" he rasped, clutching hold of my arm with a bony but tight grip.

I tried to shake him off, half-afraid of the intense look in his eyes.

"Yeah, it's just me," I whispered.

"My brother—my brother calls to me. He wants to be free. He's in so much pain—so much pain...A poor fool, misguided, as always." He shook his head, wiping away the tears.

"Is he in danger?" I asked quickly.

"He is dying."

"Tejus is *dying*?" I exclaimed, forgetting to keep my voice down.

Zerus let go of my hand abruptly.

"Tejus is dying?" he repeated, horrified.

"What? No—that's what *you* said," I replied in exasperation.

"No," he whispered, understanding dawning on him, "no. I talk of *Jenus*. It is he who needs my help—he who is so lost."

I sighed with relief. Tejus wasn't exactly my favorite person in the world, but I was glad he was safe—it probably meant the rest of GASP was too. As soon as the relief passed, I went back to questioning the sentry.

"You're communicating with Jenus?" I asked, wanting to be absolutely clear on the facts before I woke the others.

"I do not know how," Zerus replied quietly, "but he calls to me—through my mind. He whispers that he wants forgiveness, that he chose the wrong path. That he loves me."

At the mention of 'whispering' my ears pricked up—it reminded me too much of the entity, and its soft, cruel voice. Was the entity using Zerus as a weapon too?

"Does he ask you to do anything specifically?"

"He asks me to free him," the sentry replied. "That is all. But I do not know how—I only see images that he sends me, of dark shadows by the sea, and a great fortress rising up through the ground."

"Okay," I replied slowly, "I think we need to get you to Tejus. Your brother needs to know all this. The fact that you can communicate with Jenus is important. It might be able to help them somehow—I don't know."

The sentry sat up, his panic residing.

"I would like to see Tejus," he agreed. "Maybe he can help Jenus?"

"Err…maybe," I replied.

Field and Fly had told us what had happened to Jenus when they'd returned from delivering the energy-infused powers—how the entity had taken possession of his body in much the same way he had with Benedict. As Jenus had most likely been a willing subject, I doubted very much that he could now be saved.

"Anyway," I added quickly, "either way you should definitely see Tejus. I'll get one of the jinn or Hawks to take you back to Memenion's palace—is that okay?"

The sentry nodded.

I hurried to wake up Benedict and the others, while mentally kicking myself. Why hadn't we asked him earlier which brother he was mumbling about? If Jenus really was communicating with his brother it meant that somehow his consciousness must be surviving the possession—just like Benedict's had.

It meant we still had hope.

Hazel

I knocked quietly on Ruby's door. I thought she might be asleep, but she immediately pulled it open, a worried frown creasing her forehead. Of course she wouldn't be asleep. She was waiting for news like I was.

"Nothing," I said, before she could ask.

She nodded, sighing.

"How are you holding up?" she asked, gesturing for me to come in.

"Okay. It's just been a while, and we haven't heard anything..." I trailed off. There was no point in speculating. Maybe it was a good thing—maybe they'd found a way to lock the portal, which was why they were taking so long.

"I keep thinking that if there was good news they would have sent Jeriad or Lethe back," she commented, flopping down on the bed. I joined her, curling up against the headboard.

"Maybe, maybe not—it's a small team. My grandpa probably needs every one of them," I replied. I just wished that he hadn't needed Tejus.

I smiled suddenly, remembering the other reason I'd come to find her.

"I also heard rumors that you might have some news for me?" I asked, poking her with an outstretched toe.

She sat up, her face aghast.

"Oh, God—Hazel, I'm so sorry—I wanted you to be the first to know…but with everything happening…" She flung her hands up in the air, then quickly shoved one of them in front of my face.

I grabbed her hand, admiring the gold band that lay on her wedding finger.

"Oh, it's so lovely!" I sighed happily. "I'm so glad—you're a perfect match, aren't you? He's the only man I think I've ever seen stand up to you," I teased.

"Shut up." She grinned. "But yeah, pretty much. He's a good influence on me…and I'm crazy about him," she added shyly.

I laughed out loud. I'd never seen Ruby come even *close* to shy. "Wow—are you blushing?"

She tutted at me, shoving my foot away.

"It makes the waiting worse," she replied eventually, all traces of good humor gone. "The fact that he almost died—I don't know…It makes everything seem so fragile. Like you can be so completely happy, and then…"

"Don't think about it," I replied quietly, not letting on that it was pretty much the same thing I'd been thinking all evening.

She nodded. "I know. How do you think the boys and Yelena are getting on?"

"Field said they were doing okay. I just worry about them being in the forest at night. Mom and Dad are worried too, but at least they have the Hawk boys, Ridan, Aisha and Horatio with them. I just hope they find the jinn soon."

"Do you think they're still here?" Ruby asked. "I mean really? Don't you think it's strange that they've stayed away all this time—through the red rains, the ice fires, the earthquakes…If they wanted to help, surely they would have done something by now?"

"I know," I replied. "That's what I think. If they are here, maybe they don't want to help. But then it might just be a case of *forcing* them to."

"GASP can be pretty persuasive." Ruby smirked.

There was another knock on the door. We both jumped up as my mom's head appeared around the door.

"Lucas has just come through the barriers—hurry."

We ran, following my mom down the stairs, all the other

137

GASP members coming out of their rooms and joining us in total silence as we hurried to hear the verdict. Lucas reached the entrance doors before we did, Ash by his side.

"It's not great news," Lucas burst out, holding his hands up for silence, anticipating the flood of questions that would be coming his way. "Ghouls have arrived through the portal—including a ghoul queen that Ben recognized."

I looked at Ruby.

Why are ghouls coming to join the entity?

"Not only that, but the entity has taken over Hellswan castle—sort of. I'll explain the details later," Lucas continued. "It's also watching us. Right now it knows about every move we make…and has since the beginning. The others are still by the cove—we're still waiting for the right moment to get to the portal, but the shadow's been hovering over it constantly. It's going to be difficult to get close, but it won't be impossible."

"What can we do?" my mom asked.

"Be ready," Lucas replied. "We might need to go into battle again at a moment's notice. Until then, just keep the barriers secure. Has there been any more news from the boys?"

Ruby and I shook our heads.

"Not since Field left."

"Okay." Lucas nodded. "Get your weapons ready—ministers and guards too," he added to Ash. "We'll send the dragons when we need back-up."

I blinked and he was gone.

"I guess we get ready then," Ruby murmured to me. "Shall we check the armory, see if there's anything else we can bring?"

"Good idea," I agreed.

Most of the weapons down there were infused with the immortal waters. If we were going to go to battle again, I wanted more than just the dagger—as awesome as it was.

"I'm thinking arrows," I mused out loud.

"I'm thinking a *mace*," Ruby replied.

"Old school."

"Yeah, I'm going medieval on the entity's ass this time. Enough is enough."

I couldn't have agreed more.

DEREK

We joined the warlock and the rest of our party by the cliff edge. They had followed a row of jagged rock around the cove, taking them closer to the portal.

"Why haven't they attacked?" Ibrahim asked, as soon as he saw us.

"No idea," I replied. "Maybe they just don't see us as a threat right now…or the armies are playing with us—biding their time."

Not knowing the answer to that made me uncomfortable. I wasn't entirely sure what our next move should be—whether it would be sensible to leave, or continue to wait for an opportunity to get down to the portal. If the entity was underestimating us, perhaps in its arrogance, it might provide us with a chance.

"How close, physically, do you need to be to close the portal?" I asked.

Ibrahim glanced over at Nuriya.

"We're not sure," the warlock replied. "It took the stones to open it, and a great deal of power. It will take time to seal it – and if we're at a greater distance, it will be harder."

"So what do we do now?" Sherus asked impatiently.

"I'm wondering if we take our chances and attack the shadow now—maybe we call for back-up. If we could act swiftly then we might be able to give you enough time to get to the portal before the entity sends reinforcements," I replied, thinking that even if we *could* take on the shadow, the entity's response would be too swift for the warlock and jinn to accomplish their task.

"Do you think that's wise?" Nuriya looked at me steadily. "When the entity is watching everything that we do?"

I heard the sound of someone approaching behind us. I motioned for them all to be silent. A few moments later, Lucas stepped into view and crouched down behind the rocks next to me.

"How's the palace?" I asked.

"Secure. They're ready to move at a moment's notice."

I nodded my thanks, then told my brother what I was planning. Lucas seemed to accept the risk, but the fae king balked.

"This is suicide," he muttered angrily. "The shadow is waiting for us to attack. We'd be playing right into the entity's hands."

"I'm not sure we have a choice anymore," Tejus murmured. I looked over at him. His gaze was fixed on the shadow above the portal—it was moving.

"It's approaching *us*," Tejus asserted. "If we don't stand and fight, then we're done for anyway."

The sentry rose in one swift movement, unsheathing the Hellswan sword from his belt. He faced the approaching shadow, his muscles poised to strike, waiting for the black form to get close enough.

We all followed his lead. I watched as the shadow crept over the cove, leaving the portal unwatched. This was our chance.

"Ibrahim, Nuriya—try to go further around," I commanded. "See if you can reach the portal while we distract the army."

They left, vanishing entirely from view. All we needed to do was provide enough of a distraction that their magic wouldn't be noticed...we didn't know if the shadow could see behind their spells or evasion tactics. Considering the team I had with me, distraction should be an easy enough task.

Soon the gray, cloying blackness had surrounded us. I felt the strange sense of dread creep up my spine, the way it always did when the shadow was near—my theory was that the creatures tried to make us feel separate and alone, to instill a sense of hopelessness in their enemies before they struck. It was an effective strategy, unless you were facing a group of fighters who were family—or potential family, in the case of Tejus. My brother and I had seen too much together, fought side by side too many times through the centuries for us to ever feel that we didn't have one another's back. We knew we did, and we always would.

Tejus was the first to make a direct hit on the encroaching shadow. The form of the soldier appeared, its ashen face twisted in pain and fury before it turned to smoke-like ashes.

The battle had begun.

I ripped my claws into the dark smoke. I wounded one of them, but he reached out and grabbed me around the neck, claws digging into me, his strength at odds with his shadowy appearance. I struggled against the vice he created, one hand prying off his grip, the other retrieving an immortal water-infused dagger from my belt. Before he became aware of what I was doing, I slashed the dagger upward along his chest. He bellowed—a sound that didn't seem like it had just come from him, but the entire army. In the next moment he was ash, and another bit of shadow moved in to take his place.

I swiftly glanced over at my son. He and Tejus were taking on groups at a time. Back to back, they spun swords at a rapid speed, their aim at neck height—the heads of the soldiers flying upward a split second before their bodies crumbled to nothing.

They actually looked like they were enjoying themselves, and they weren't the only ones. Lucas and Aiden seemed to be reveling in the attack, using claws (in Aiden's case) and swords to cast fatal blows at the enemy. Lethe attacked from above, bellowing ice to freeze the shadow, swooping down to snap at shoulders and heads, then dropping them back onto the ground. It was an effective method of attack, but it still wasn't enough. The shadow continued to grow; for each dead ashen soldier, another would appear in its place. I continued to slice through my fair share, conscious of keeping one eye on the portal, waiting for a sign that Ibrahim and Nuriya were making progress.

The shadow wasn't slowing down. Like the last battle, it didn't seem to be getting much smaller in size no matter what we did.

Once again, I contemplated calling for back-up, telling Lethe to fetch the others to help. Before I could, I heard the rumbling of an army moving toward us. It was coming from the direction of Hellswan.

The entity and its queen were on their way.

BEN

I heard the rest of the army approaching along the path. Tejus
tensed behind me, causing him to falter, a blow from his sword
coming just a second too late. I could hear the sharp intake of
his breath as the creature took a swipe at his arm before Tejus
lashed out in fury, annihilating the soldier.

I was facing the path that led to Hellswan. It was difficult
with the mass of shadow in front of me, but I could see the glare
of the flaming branches that the ghouls were carrying, and the
strange, translucent blue glow their skin gave off under the
moonlight.

We were already surrounded by the shadow. If we had to
stand and fight the rest of them, we were over. I kept battling,

but my breathing had become uneven. I was starting to feel afraid. I didn't want this to be my last moment. I wanted to see River, Grace and Field. I couldn't leave my family; I'd promised River that I'd return.

"What do we do?" I called to my dad, knowing he would have heard their approach too.

"I'm thinking," my dad roared, decapitating the head of another soldier. He tried to position himself so he could get a better look at the shoreline. I wasn't able to see Ibrahim or Nuriya, or if they'd had any success yet in closing the portal.

"The portal?" I asked, calling out to the whole team—Lethe had a better view than any of us.

"Nothing's happening," the ice dragon called back.

Dammit.

If the entity and the rest of the army were heading this way, then we'd failed on all counts.

The screeching of the ghouls grew louder.

"Tejus! Ben!" my dad bellowed in our direction. "If things get…tricky, head back to the palace. I mean it—just get the hell out of here, okay?"

I agreed with him, and so did Tejus. But I knew that neither of us would leave. I wasn't blind—I could see, even from the limited time we'd spent with the sentries, that Tejus was crazy about my niece, but he was also a warrior. One who wouldn't leave his men behind.

I guess this is it, then.

The rest of the army kept drawing closer. In a few minutes, I would see them come into full view on the path, and then they would be upon us—a force that we couldn't even hope to destroy.

"Lethe." My dad caught the dragon's attention. "Go and get backup. We need the rest of the army—"

The dragon roared in shock before my father could finish his order. I looked up to see his talons gripped around the head of one of the soldiers, a large and vicious-looking rip in his wing.

"Lethe!" I yelled, rushing forward as swiftly as I could to slice away the shadow that was rearing upward to drag the dragon down. Tejus joined me, and together we slashed at the darkness as Lethe disposed of the soldier in his grip.

He landed back on the ground, breathing ice and snapping at the shadow.

"Can you still fly?" I yelled.

"Not sure," he replied. "I need to give it a few moments." He fought on, just as deadly on the ground as he was in the air. My father turned to Sherus.

"Go and tell the others, we need back up, *now!*"

The fae king vanished instantly, while the rest of us fought on.

"If we're not going to make it," Tejus growled, "then I want to take as many of these down with me as I can. Are you with me?"

"I'm in," I replied.

In the next moment, the ghouls were upon us. They dodged through the shadow, screaming, claws out and mouths open. They were easy to kill in comparison, but their sheer number made fighting both species at once nearly impossible.

I heard the laughter of the entity in my head once again.

My children will finish you off, while I finish the worlds you hold so dear.

I spun around to try to see if I could find Jenus, maybe to end this once and for all. Instead, the shadow thickened around me and a strong force—like one of the sentries' barriers—blew me backwards. I went flying into Tejus. Both of us were knocked to the floor. My head slammed into the earth, my sight spinning while I urged my body to get up. The force of the blow affected my hearing. I crawled to my knees, the ground spinning beneath me, but all I could hear was silence.

"Tejus? Dad?" I tried to call out, but I couldn't hear myself. I looked over to see Tejus scrambling toward his sword, looking as disorientated as I did.

The shadow backed away, and I saw the rest of our group, all struggling to stand, looking around in confusion and anger.

The shadow moved down between the narrow path to the cove. My first thought was of Ibrahim and Nuriya, down by the portal. I staggered forward, using my hands to clamber over to the edge of the cliff.

Nuriya and Ibrahim were trying to make the shadow and the ghouls back off by surrounding themselves with ice fire. It was working on the ghouls—they screeched around the edges, burning themselves when they tried to get close. It wasn't as effective on the shadow, and they kept having to vanish and reappear to keep the black mass from consuming them.

Jenus and the ghoul queen were fast approaching the portal, and I tried to call out a warning.

I was too late.

Ibrahim and Nuriya were sent scattering by a barrier expelled by Jenus. From this vantage point I could see what was happening more clearly. We too had been hit by a strange force-field, nothing like the translucent glows that the sentries created as barriers, but something stronger, darker. The edges of it burned red, and rather than being transparent, it was the same graying tones as the shadow.

They were knocked unconscious.

I called out in rage, frustrated by my own helplessness. Jenus and his queen stepped toward the yawning portal, and then they were gone—the ghouls and the shadow following close behind.

We had failed.

The entity had just been released out into the world.

BENEDICT

It was dawn when we finally sent Zerus off with Field. Julian had woken me in the night, telling me what the sentry had been trying to say all along, that Jenus was the brother who had been communicating with him all this time.

I was furious with myself for missing that vital piece of information, and I could tell Julian was too. We woke the jinn and Yelena, and then called for the Hawk boys and Ridan. They had been keeping watch over us from the trees above, and were ready to take him then and there, but Zerus, in his befuddled state, suddenly became terrified of returning to Tejus and the ministers. It took forever to calm him down. He refused all help from the jinn, seemingly more terrified by their strange appearance this morning than he was last night. He was in a *bad* way. Yelena was the most helpful—she spoke to him for a while, both of them sitting by the re-lit fire, murmuring to one another, while we all paced in agitation, wondering if Aisha or Horatio should get Tejus *here* instead.

Eventually, whatever Yelena had been telling him worked. Reluctantly he let Field carry him—they would fly back to Memenion's palace and tell Tejus what was going on.

The rest of us got moving. Now we had no guide to take us to the base of the mountain, we relied heavily on Sky, Fly and Ridan to guide us. As we got closer and could see the structure of the mountain range more clearly, the jinn seemed hopeful that we would find some of their kind hiding out in the small caves that dotted the multiple rock faces. We sent the Hawk boys and the dragon on ahead, hoping their keen eyesight would locate anything that looked out of place. They hovered over the face of the mountain – slowly tracking across its surface so they didn't miss anything.

As we began to climb, finding pathways as best we could, Julian slipped on a loose stone and swore.

"Look," he said once he'd regained his balance, "this is so stupid. Let's just wait here, there's no point killing ourselves. If Ridan and the Hawks find anything, they can come and get us."

"I agree with Julian," Yelena called out behind me, before I could say anything. "I don't see why we need to walk the whole way. Their eyesight is much better than ours, I don't see how we can be of that much help."

"Aisha, Horatio, what do you think?" I asked, remembering my grandfather's advice about a good leader always listening to the rest of his team.

Aisha looked up at the mountain, hands on her hips as she studied it. "It's easier for Horatio and me – we can travel much faster than you can. If the Hawks and Ridan could point out areas of interest to us, it might make this faster."

"Don't worry, Benedict," Horatio added, seeing my downcast expression, "we'll cover the mountain—we'll make sure we find them. We won't come back to GASP empty-handed."

"All right," I agreed. "We'll wait for you, Ridan and the Hawks then."

I sat down on the nearest rock, annoyed to be out of action but realizing it was probably for the best.

"I hope we find them quickly." Yelena broke the silence, chewing on her bottom lip and looking worriedly out across the forest. I didn't reply. I had started thinking about what might be happening back at the castle and the cove – how much danger my family and the other members of GASP were in. I really hoped that the discovery of Zerus and Jenus's communication would help them.

I jumped slightly when Aisha appeared beside me.

"We've found something, quick!" she said, and in an instant we'd vanished off the face of the rock. I blinked once, and suddenly we were standing at the top of the mountain – the whole of Nevertide at our feet.

At the apex of the final rock formation, there was a small opening, its interior cast in gloom. Next to it grew a single tree, low and small, with gnarled and twisted roots that had been battered down by wind. Hanging from one of its four branches was what looked like an old tin lantern.

Sky, Fly, Horatio and Ridan had waited for us. We all fell silent as we approached the opening, each on our guard as we prepared to face what might lie within. Before we could get within a few feet of our destination, a voice echoed from within the cave.

"I saw that you were coming. But you are a little late, I'm afraid."

We glanced at one another in surprise. The voice was frail—female, and quite wispy—almost as if we were hearing the sounds of a ghost or some other disembodied creature.

I stepped closer to the cave, wondering if we'd found what we were looking for, or if it was another bewildered sentry hermit.

I heard a rustling noise, and a woman appeared, stepping out from the shadows into the morning light. Her body was stooped, but straightened up as she left the low ceiling of the cave. I stepped back. Not because she seemed threatening, but I was startled by her appearance. I half felt like I should have bowed down or something…She looked so *mystical*, like a princess or something. Despite her height, she was very frail-looking, her body like a reed in the wind, and her skin so pale it seemed to glow.

Her eyes fixed on mine, and I stopped breathing. Her irises were blue but so pale they were almost white, and she seemed to look *past* me, like I was a phantom. Her hair was long, almost touching the ground, and as white as snow. She wore a white dress too—a plain sheath of material that wrapped around her shapeless body, making it almost impossible to tell how old she was. The weirdest thing about her was her skin. Aside from it being so pale, black shapes or symbols moved across it, flickering in and out of view like shadows. I became transfixed by their movement, but she didn't seem to mind or notice that she was being stared at.

"W-what do you mean we're late?" Yelena asked eventually, her voice slightly trembling.

"You are late finding me." She sighed. "But it doesn't matter…time is turning as it wills, and the pieces of the story are falling where they should."

"I don't understand," I replied, hoping that I wouldn't offend her.

She smiled hesitantly—as if she wasn't really used to doing it.

I wondered how long she'd been up here by herself…or even if she *was* alone.

"I am what you've been seeking. The creator of the stones, the one who banished the entity."

"We were under the impression that you were a jinni, and that there would be more of you," Aisha interrupted, frowning at the woman. She seemed less than impressed by her appearance—the only one of us who was.

The woman shook her head. "There is just me."

"What *are* you?" I asked.

"I am half jinn, on my mother's side, and half-Ancient, on my father's side," she replied, her voice lilting with pleasure.

"A-An Ancient?" Aisha gasped.

"Yes," the woman replied, apparently surprised at the jinni's tone.

"*And* you're an Oracle," Aisha asserted furiously. "I recognize those symbols from the dead Oracle twins, but… you can't possibly be the lovechild of an *Ancient* and a jinni—even regular witches and jinn are sworn enemies and practically never mingle, not to speak of *Ancients* and the jinn of old. They would have attacked each other on sight! You're lying to us."

The woman instantly looked troubled, and hurt. I balled my hands into fists, my chest tightening. Suddenly I wasn't so convinced by her innocent and harmless appearance—I'd heard all about the Ancients, of course. They were an evil group of witches that used to rule The Sanctuary more than a thousand years ago. One of them who'd managed to survive, Lilith, had been the bane of my family's existence, particularly my mother's and Uncle Ben's, for a significant amount of time—the evil old hag had wanted their blood. It was Kiev we had to thank for eventually ending her, after an extremely difficult struggle. I couldn't imagine how powerful this creature might be... I had never heard of an Ancient conceiving an Oracle.

"We don't mean to offend you," Yelena mumbled, not understanding what was going on. She obviously felt sorry for the woman and glared at me, waiting for me to say something that might make her feel more at ease.

"I am an Oracle," the woman replied. "I see the past, the future and the present."

"Oh, I thought you were blind," Yelena burst out before she could stop herself. She covered her mouth in horror before continuing, "I'm so sorry—it's just there was a girl at my school—and she had eyes like you, and she was blind—and I thought that..."

"I am blind," the woman interrupted her gently, "but it doesn't mean that I can't see."

Yelena nodded her head slowly, still very confused.

"So, if you're an Oracle and part Ancient and Jinni, what are you doing in Nevertide? How did you even get here?" Aisha demanded.

"This is my home," she replied softly. "I have lived nowhere else. I watch the worlds from my mountain—it's peaceful here."

I was starting to get a bit angry...or, actually, *furious*. If she had been here all this time—watching everything like she claimed—why hadn't she done anything?

"You haven't helped!" I burst out. "Nevertide's been falling to pieces, and you haven't done a thing. Why not? If you locked the entity and its army in the stones in the first place, why didn't you just do it again? Loads of people have died! I got possessed— and it was really crap!"

The Oracle looked at me, her expression sad, like a wounded animal.

"I'm so sorry, but things must be this way. It is not true that I have not helped—I have intervened to the extent I could. I have maintained the dome that surrounds this land to keep Nevertide cut off from the rest of the supernatural world, I sent the warning signs as I promised I would, and I gave Tejus of Hellswan the opportunity to rise to power by building the labyrinth of the dead emperor, so that Tejus's mettle might be tested against his brothers'. Had I not offered my services to the Emperor when I saw that Jenus would have automatically been his father's choice, and offered to help him put his sons to the test instead – Nevertide would have been destroyed. If you could but see the events that have not unfolded, you would be thanking me—not treating me like a monster."

I was starting to feel a little bad, but there were still so many things that I didn't understand. The Oracle looked like she was about to start crying, and I nudged Yelena—*say something!*

Yelena shook her head in panic, looking devastated that we'd managed to get off to such a bad start.

"Tell us about the dome," Horatio prompted, his voice a fraction more gentle than Aisha's. "You said you maintained it—who created it in the first place?"

"My parents did. They found this land for me a long, long time ago. It was empty—there were a few ghouls here, and some other creatures like goblins and nymphs, but they never bothered me. I liked the nymphs…" She sighed sadly. "But then more ghouls came, and then the humans—and I decided to intervene after the first war. That's when I locked the entity away."

"But what is the entity?" I asked, confused that she was only referring to ghouls.

"I suppose you could call him the original ghoul," she murmured. "The first—along with his army. They are a very different breed than the others, far more powerful, with several differing traits, and they have been around since the dawn of time… the darkness to any light."

We were all silent. I couldn't believe that the ghouls I'd seen were the same as the shadow and the entity—or, at the least, the same species. Ghouls were gross and horrible, but they didn't terrify me as much as the shadow, or seem to have the same amount of power.

"We need to take you to GASP," I replied hoarsely.

"Wait," Aisha snapped. "I want to know why your parents trapped you here. Did they think you were a danger? Was it a punishment?"

Now the Oracle looked mortally offended. For the first time since we'd interrogated her, she looked angry. She fixed her unseeing white eyes on Aisha.

"You can be cold and unfeeling, Aisha of the Nasiri Jinn. You are lucky to have Horatio Drizan to rub away some of your sharper edges. My parents put me here to protect me. As you rightly said, the Ancients and the jinn would not have looked gladly on my parents' union. They loved me, and my being here is an act of love."

Aisha looked a little shamefaced, and shut up, but still eyed her speculatively. I didn't think Aisha trusted the Oracle one bit...and to be honest, I didn't blame her. From what I knew of the Oracle twins, the Ancients and even most of the jinn, her heritage wasn't exactly the most comforting mix. Even so, we needed to get her back to GASP and the sentries.

"Will you help us now?" I asked, hoping that she wouldn't just vanish thanks to Aisha's blunt tongue.

She smiled faintly at me.

"There is no more help to be given, but I see that you won't understand that. I will come to see your tribe, human. There is gray there...I can't see clearly. Some things have not been decided."

What does that mean?

"About the entity? Will we win the battle?" I asked eagerly.

"You can 'win', as you say. If nothing changes from the current course of action. But I see that you are resourceful. You took the flowers my parents created for me—the ones that I used to create the stones. That was clever."

"So you don't *know*?" I clarified. What was the point of an Oracle if they couldn't predict anything?

"The future is flexible; it changes as the wind does. There is nothing sure in this life except perhaps the passing of time, and even that is malleable..." She sighed with contentment, as if that fact pleased her greatly for some reason.

"But you'll come back with us?" I asked, wanting to get back to a conversation that made even the slightest bit of sense.

"Yes, but like I say, it is too late."

I looked at the rest of the team. They shrugged, no one really knowing what to say. Aisha rolled her eyes.

"Horatio and I will travel back with her," she snapped.

I took one last look at the Oracle before stepping into the arms of Sky. She looked nervous, and I wondered if her reaction was due to the possibility of coming face-to-face with the entity, or GASP.

I supposed we would soon find out.

HAZEL

Ash, Ruby and I were waiting by the barriers when Sherus arrived. He looked pale and exhausted, perspiration forming at the hairline of his copper waves, his clear amber eyes troubled.

"Derek sent me," he stated. "They're waiting for you back at the cove. The entity and the ghoul queen have departed through the portal—we are afraid that Tejus's vision is beginning. We need to leave for Earth and the In-Between."

"Is Tejus okay?" I asked.

"No casualties, though Lethe was injured. But I believe he'll survive."

"We're ready to move," Ash said.

We were. Ever since Lucas had passed along the message, Ash

had been ensuring that GASP, the guards and the ministers were as well armed as they could be. We had sent Azaiah, Blue and Rock to the Impartial Ministers' monastery to collect more of the water. Sixteen guards now had barrels strapped to their backs, full of the deadly liquid.

The children and the villagers would be marching down to the cove with us. It was too dangerous to leave them in the palace—if they had a chance to escape through the portal, they should be allowed to take it. Otherwise, if we failed, they would be left in Nevertide at the mercy of the entity. We had given some of the older kids weapons, and they had vowed to protect the younger ones. The villagers were all fully armed too, more ready and willing to fight to the death than we'd given them credit for. The rage they'd expressed toward Tejus when the first earthquakes had struck was now entirely focused on the entity and his armies. They wanted their freedom, and they were willing to pay the price.

We started to march, the dragons and the Hawks flying ahead along with the ministers who were using vultures, and the rest of us either running or riding on bull-horses. I wondered how we were all going to travel through the portal, and hoped that we had enough witches and jinn to pull it off. If Tejus's vision was correct, then we'd be traveling to multiple places within Europe—along with a journey to the In-Between.

"Are you ready?" Ruby asked me as we rode out of the

barriers.

"Hell, yeah," I replied. "I want us to end this today. I want to go *home*..." The word caught in my throat, physically choking me. It had been so *long*. I would have thought that having all my loved ones around me would totally eradicate any feelings of homesickness, but it wasn't the case. I missed the familiar smells, my own bed—the peaceful waters, the redwoods, the lake, *everything*.

"Homesick?" Ruby asked gently.

"Yeah," I replied. "You?"

She looked over at Ash, riding on the other side of her. She turned back to me, her eyes soft and thoughtful.

"Not as much as I thought I'd be."

I nodded. I got it. I gave my bull-horse a gentle kick. If Ash and Ruby were going to stay in Nevertide and make it their home, then I was going to make damned sure that there wasn't a shadow, a ghoul or an entity in sight.

When we reached the top of the cove, I caught sight of Tejus up ahead, and my heart leapt. Even from this distance I could see that he looked exhausted—he looked like a panther after a hunt, waiting to go off somewhere and lick his wounds. Ignoring the rest of the army behind me, I veered away from the procession and rode up to him. The bull-horse had barely come to a stop before I jumped off, launching myself in his arms. He grabbed me fiercely, his strength taking the breath from my body. There was so much that I wanted to say to him in that moment, some sentiment that would let him know that I loved him with everything I had, but I just couldn't find the words. I pushed my feelings toward him, lights and colors that painted them better than I could speak them. He rested his forehead against mine, letting his own thoughts and emotions flow back into me, everything swirling together in technicolor.

"Tejus!" my grandpa barked.

I stepped back, and Tejus grinned at me.

"I'm coming!" he roared, grabbing my hand. We made our way over to the GASP members, standing with Ash and Ruby.

"I'm going to divide the teams up," my grandpa instructed us. "We can't afford to stay together—won't get there in time. From Tejus's visions it's likely that the entity is going to focus its own efforts on one location, sending its shadow army, the ghouls and the queen elsewhere. Sofia, Rose and I discussed the locations using Hazel's description. I think we're looking at Paris, Brussels, Berlin, London, and of course the In-Between. The fire planet. Each team will get a full briefing on the exact locations—Hazel, will you do that?"

I nodded, frantically trying to recapture the memories of the mind-meld Tejus and I had shared…what if I left out a detail and sent them to the wrong place? Thousands of people could die! Ruby's arm brushed up against mine and she smiled reassuringly.

You've got this, her expression said.

I inhaled a breath, trying to calm down.

"Each team will be assigned a leader," my grandfather continued, "and each team will be assigned at least one witch or jinni to assist with transportation. As soon as any of you come into contact with the entity, those who can portal easily need to be sent to find me and my team—we will consolidate our attack. I think, or rather, I *hope*, that the shadow is going to lose power once the entity is destroyed. Vivienne, you're leading the Paris team; Kiev, Brussels; Ben, In-Between; Bastien, you will lead the London team; and I will lead the Berlin team. Team leaders, speak to Hazel, and I will organize the rest of your team members."

I stood back, suddenly confronted with expectant faces all looking in my direction. My great-aunt Vivienne was the first to approach, her intense blue-violet eyes latching on to mine. "Tell me everything you know—don't leave out any of the details."

I nodded. Taking another deep breath, I started to describe what I'd seen. Tejus approached halfway through, helping me fill in some of the details that I'd missed. Next came Kiev, Bastien, then Sherus and Ben who wanted to double-check the location of the vision, and finally my grandpa, who brought my mom with him—she'd spent some time in Berlin on a mission, and could remember it well.

I felt light-headed when I'd finished.

"Grandpa." I stopped him before he could walk away. "Whose team am I on?"

"You're with me." He smiled.

I nodded a thank you. *Huh.* Fighting side-by-side with the famous Derek Novak?

Benedict would have a fit when he heard…which reminded me—somehow we needed to get word to my brother and the others that we were leaving Nevertide. I didn't like the idea of him remaining here without us. I'd always envisioned us walking out of here together, having finally made it, despite the odds stacked against us.

When Tejus and I walked over to my mom and dad, they were already discussing it with my grandpa.

"We'll send the other Hawk boys to tell them," he agreed. 'The important thing is that they keep searching—and hurry. Using the stones might be the only way to trap the entity; if that's the case…"

My mom placed her hand on my grandpa's arm, stopping him from finishing the sentence.

"We know," she said firmly, "but they won't fail—and neither will we."

I turned away from my parents. I hoped my mom was right.

"You're fighting with us too, right?" I asked Tejus. I had assumed that he would be—my grandpa tried his best not to split up families and friends during a battle, though often it was unavoidable.

"Like I'd let it be any other way," he muttered. I knew he wasn't pleased that I'd be fighting, but there was nothing he could do about it.

I looked at Tejus. "I can't wait for you to meet the twenty-first century." I laughed, thinking more of Tejus's old-fashioned values than the cities we'd be traveling to. He would have seen some of Earth's urban areas before anyway, but perhaps only from a distance.

"If you think a dimension change will stop me from being so over-protective, you're sadly mistaken," he replied dryly.

"I wouldn't have it any other way."

I meant it. As much as I valued my independence, knowing that Tejus was watching my back as I was watching his made me feel safe—no matter what the danger. I hoped that would never change between us.

TEJUS

We waited for the teams to be assembled, and the villagers and human children to be ushered out of immediate sight at the opposite end of the cove, moving them as far away from the rotting corpses of the dead Acolytes as we could. When the guards arrived, I would ask them to set the bodies on fire – we didn't have time to hold proper funerals. I knew that Ash was worried about the safety of the villagers, but if we needed to get them out of Nevertide quickly, the cove was the best place for them. I had other concerns—mainly that we were putting a lot of faith in the visions I'd had. I still wasn't convinced they weren't some kind of trick, images placed in my mind by the entity to mislead us. I'd shared my thoughts with Derek while we'd waited for the rest of GASP and the sentries to arrive. The vampire felt that, as it was the only lead we had, we should follow up on it, otherwise we'd be traveling from continent to continent across Earth without any direction. It would take too long. I had agreed, eventually, but I still couldn't shake my misgivings.

I watched Blue and Rock, the two Hawk boys, fly off into the distance in search of Benedict and the others. As soon as they disappeared from view, I noticed with curiosity that one of them appeared to be returning—a black dot in the distance growing steadily larger.

"Do you think he forgot something?" Hazel asked, coming to stand next to me as we gazed up at the sky.

"Maybe he wants to join us—I suppose it doesn't take the two of them to deliver the message."

"I don't know," Hazel replied doubtfully, "the Hawk boys tend to stick together. I'd be surprised if one of them would be willing to go off into battle without the others voluntarily."

As the dot became larger, I started to notice that there were two people approaching. They were still too far away to distinguish who it was, but the Hawk boy was carrying someone—probably a male sentry, judging by the size, who was dressed in the red cloak of Hellswan. I used True Sight to get a better idea of who the sentry was, and as I honed in on the Hawk, I realized that it was Field—the boy with the long dark hair, related to Ben. In his arms, he was carrying Zerus.

"Are you seeing what I am?" Hazel breathed.

Seeing my brother for the first time since the earthquakes brought up mixed emotions. I had truly presumed that he was dead, slowly adjusting to the idea that aside from Jenus, I was the only Hellswan left. I was glad to see him—and I was glad that out of all my brothers, he was the one who had survived. Zerus had always been the nicest, kindest and quietest one of all of us, happier in his room with his telescope, watching the stars, than he was with the business of the kingdom or Nevertide politics.

How he had survived in the first place was astonishing. I wondered if he'd gotten out of the castle long before its collapse—or managed to escape unnoticed while the mayhem ensued. Either way, it was strange that he hadn't sought me out prior to now. Did I need to be as wary of this brother as I was of Jenus?

The crowds of GASP members and sentries parted as Field landed. He released my brother, who stumbled forward, looking around at us all with wide eyes, his hands clasped together. He was nervous.

"Zerus." I greeted him with a nod, not sure how comfortable he would be with an embrace. He seemed even more skittish than usual.

"T-Tejus," he stammered, and then fell silent.

Field looked from one of us to the other, and then cleared his throat awkwardly.

"We found Zerus in the Dauoa forests. Benedict believed he could help us find a path through the mountains, but we soon discovered that he was receiving messages from Jenus. We thought we should bring him to you."

I stared at my brother in astonishment.

"Is this true, Zerus?" I barked, trying to get his full attention. His eyes continued to dart across the assembled members of GASP, clearly taken aback by their strangeness.

When it was clear that he wasn't going to speak, I tried to put him at ease.

"These are Hazel's friends and family, they're here to help us end the entity and its armies. You know of the threat we face, I assume?"

Zerus nodded.

"I have seen the shadow. I have seen the darkness," he mumbled.

"So tell me what Jenus has said," I encouraged, trying to keep my impatience in check. We were running out of time, and I could sense that I wasn't the only one who wanted to shake the information out of my brother.

"He speaks to me in my dreams," Zerus whispered. "Begging forgiveness and absolution. He cries that his master tricked him, that his soul dies more every day, and that he wishes to be free from his enslavement. He shows me images of Earth, of humans in great pain, running in terror from the armies of the entity."

I glanced at Derek. The vision I had must have been sent by Jenus somehow, perhaps using the power of the entity to mind-meld with me at such a distance. If Jenus was still 'alive' despite the entity residing within him, then it would explain the barrier that Hazel and I had created—why we had felt that there had been another form of energy there aside from our own. Had it been my brother all along, providing what help he could?

"You are sure of this? You are sure that it is Jenus and not the entity playing tricks?" I asked, wondering if the same thought had occurred to my brother.

"No." Zerus shook his head. "I am not sure. I am not sure at all—before all this our brother was cruel, a darkness inside him that blossomed with the lavish attentions of our father. It could all be a trick, but I cannot ignore the earnestness of his voice—the cries that haunt me, begging for me to free him."

I nodded, feeling pity for Zerus. It must have been difficult, alone in the forest with the pleas of Jenus haunting him. I wondered why I had not heard the same, why our brother had not tried to reach me through his own voice as he'd done with Zerus. Did he think that I would turn my back on him, ignore his cries for help?

"Why did you not tell us this sooner?" I asked eventually.

Zerus clasped his hands even tighter, the knuckles turning

white with the pressure.

"I vowed I would not return to Hellswan," he murmured. "The end was coming—the end of our time on this land, and I wanted to spend my last days alone with the stars and the silence. Forgive me, brother."

I stared at him, not knowing how to react. In the past, I would have dismissed him as a coward. I was angry at his reticence—receiving this news earlier would have perhaps enabled us to use it to our advantage—but I understood his reasons. I could not hate him for his attempts at self-preservation; our selfishness was a family trait, clearly, and I couldn't blame him for a fault that was so alive in me.

"Get some rest," I bit out.

Zerus nodded, and Field escorted him to a quiet spot away from the waiting armies, before leaving to return to his brothers. The sentries, particularly those who had resided at Hellswan, whispered to one another as he passed, but they did not speak to him.

I turned my attentions to the matter at hand.

"More proof that the visions are genuine," I observed to Derek. "This is good news."

"Indeed," the vampire replied, his blue eyes following my brother as he sat down on a rock, his cloak pulled tightly around him. "If Jenus has been trying to communicate with the two of you it must mean he's semi-conscious, or has moments of lucidity. Which leads me to believe that the entity is not as powerful as we first thought, *or* that it is spreading its power too thin."

I agreed with the latter. If the entity was maintaining the energy of the shadow army and manipulating the body of Jenus, then its powers would be unfocused. No wonder it had only appeared in battle at certain times—it was holding back, allowing its armies to do the work.

"So really, it's similar to what it did with Benedict—just a stronger form of possession?" Hazel asked.

"I think so."

"Then let's hunt it down," she replied. "Let's find a way to expose that weakness."

Derek smiled at his granddaughter. "I couldn't have put it better myself. Let's move out."

He gave the order; the sentries and the GASP members divided into their assigned teams, and we all moved toward the portal.

It was time to hunt down my brother.

DEREK

Corrine led us down into the portal. We followed the tunnel of blueish-gray swirling mists, strong air suction pulling us along the portal till we saw the uncharacteristically blue, sunshine skies that covered the North Sea. I followed after Corrine, clasping Sofia's hand; Rose, Caleb, Tejus, Hazel, Ashley and Landis followed behind us, and behind them, twenty sentry guards and ministers who would be fighting alongside us. Once we reached the ocean, Corrine held us suspended in the air. She muttered a few words under her breath, and a moment later we were standing on a wide road that faced the six columns of the Brandenburg Gate.

Tejus and the rest of the sentries looked around them in

amazement—I'd forgotten that their kind had little experience with witches, and the powers they possessed. Tejus glanced over at Corrine, half impressed, half mistrusting. Corrine smiled warmly back at him while Hazel hid a small smirk.

Either side of us, completely obscuring the lush greenery of the park on both sides of the road, were hundreds of tourist buses, each with a capacity nearing seventy. The crowds that had gathered at the base of the gates were huge, and no doubt there would be more of them in the huge courtyard on the other side of the structure.

"It's swamped," Sofia murmured, her forehead creasing into a frown.

"I don't see anything yet," I muttered. "Maybe there's time to clear the area."

"Maybe I can do something," Corrine added. "I can probably invoke a spell that would make them *think* of leaving, something that would repel them…but it would take a little time."

I thought about the witch's suggestion. I wasn't sure if we had time for a spell that subtle—we needed something that would make them move immediately.

"Corrine, can you do something to get their attention? Maybe bust the alarms on these vehicles?" I gestured to the rows of tourist coaches.

"Certainly," she replied. A moment later we were all deafened by the sounds of high-pitched alarms erupting from each of the coaches.

"Let's get moving," I yelled over the noise, pointing toward the gate.

A couple of overweight men with wrap-around shades were running toward the coaches, but it hadn't had the impact I'd wanted. We kept moving toward the gate—the tourists were dispersing too slowly.

"What else can we do?" Ashley asked.

"I think we're too late," I replied slowly. I'd stopped dead in the street, watching a dark formation creep up on the skyline, suddenly darkening the statue of the chariot rider perched atop the iconic gate.

The hopeless feeling that always accompanied the shadow started to crawl up my spine. I heard children crying—they were probably most susceptible to the feelings that the shadow projected, perhaps thinking that their parents had abandoned them, or suddenly consumed with the most basic instinct of fear.

We ran up to the columns. The shadow was growing in size, blocking out the sun completely. The screaming started, men and women running from the tourist spot in fear, not knowing what they were afraid of, just that they were.

"Corrine?" I asked.

"On it," she replied.

Our core group started to float upward, moving through the air, gaining on the shadow. She dropped us down on top of the columns of the gate, four of us either side of the chariot. Corrine remained below with the rest of the sentries. She must have been putting a spell on the tourists—they kept running, but their screaming and horrific cries of fear were starting to fade.

"What are you waiting for?" Caleb growled, his arms open and ready to receive the shadow. It worked. The form stopped spreading out toward the gardens, and focused on us.

"Hold your weapons," I called, waiting for the shadow to get close enough that we could do some damage. The black mist approached, its cloying wisps like tentacles as it reached out toward us.

"NOW!"

Tejus's sword sliced through the mass, the first soldier roaring with rage as it burst into a million ash-like pieces. After that, the shadow didn't let up. We fought furiously—each of us tearing the mists with our teeth, claws ripping at its shapeless form.

Each time the mists tried to creep around the sides and surround us from behind, furious gusts of wind, created by Corrine, pushed them back, ensuring that we were only facing the enemy head-on. It meant that the ministers and guards were useless for now—they waited below, ready to pick up the slack should one of us be wounded.

I fought with two immortal water-infused swords for better reach, and it was only Caleb who refused any man-made weapons, destroying only with his natural abilities. I noticed with pride how expertly Sofia wielded a razor-sharp whip that she'd brought with us from The Shade, slashing the shadow with perfect aim, taking out three or four of the entity's soldiers with each flick of her wrist.

Finally, I felt that we were battling our enemy with some degree of success. I knew that the shadow would keep coming until we found and destroyed the entity, but we would have to remain defending the city until it was located. I just hoped it was sooner rather than later. As I fought, I kept my eye out for Jenus and I could see Tejus doing the same thing, but he was nowhere to be seen.

"Derek!" Corrine shouted at me from down below.

I dodged the outstretched arm of a soldier, narrowly avoiding getting my face ripped to shreds.

The witch belatedly realized that her shout had been a mistake, a distraction, and appeared next to me, her own sword unsheathed and moving swiftly as she joined me in battle.

"Ibrahim just appeared. Jenus has been spotted in the In-Between. We need to go there—now. He's moving off to tell the others."

"Good," I replied, slashing through the mist with renewed vigor. "But some of us are going to need to stay here and keep the shadow at bay. Ashley, Landis!" I called. "We've found Jenus in the In-Between. I need you to stay with the sentries and keep fighting. Whatever you do, don't let the shadow leave the immediate area. If we're successful, you'll know—I'm hoping the shadow will vanish completely or weaken enough that it stops expanding."

"Got it," Landis yelled back. "Give him hell!"

I grimaced darkly. *We will,* I vowed. The entity would be sent back from whence it came.

"Are you ready?" Corrine asked.

"We're ready," I confirmed. We all linked ourselves to one another.

A split second later we were standing in the snowy peaks of Mount Logan, some of us still swinging our weapons in the direction of the vanished enemy.

"What in Nevertide?" Tejus burst out, looking around, stunned at the abrupt change in surroundings.

"Welcome to GASP." Sofia smiled at him. "Don't worry—you'll get used to it."

GRACE

Shayla looked around the Champ de Mars, squinting her large eyes in the bright sunlight.

"We need shade," Vivienne reminded the witch as she and Xavier moved beneath the natural shade of a nearby tree.

It was very peaceful here. Far off in the distance, I could hear the sound of traffic and the bustling streets of Paris, but where we were, surrounded by elegant gardens and beautifully graveled pathways, only a few people ambled past, glancing at us in surprise as they took in the tall sentry guards and ministers who had accompanied us, along with our strange outfits and heavy weaponry. Most of the sentries were muttering among themselves, looking over at Shayla with varying degrees of alarm and surprise.

Once the shade was cast over those who needed it, we moved forward, heading in the direction of the Eiffel Tower, its iconic steel structure awe-inspiring.

"Wish we were here under different circumstances..." I smiled at my husband.

"Don't worry," Lawrence said, "if we defeat the entity before dinner, I'll take you out."

I laughed, taking his hand. I couldn't imagine the shadow appearing here—it was just too much of a perfect day. I started to wonder if we had the right place, and I sensed Shayla and Lucas were thinking the same.

Before they could question Vivienne, the gravel on the path started to tremble. It was only slight at first, but it quickly increased, the ground shaking violently, causing traffic horns to blast out and loud cursing in French to erupt throughout the garden. The day didn't seem so peaceful anymore.

Screams came from the direction of the tower, but I was sure they weren't human. My instinct was proven correct a second later, when a flood of ghouls shot through the air toward us.

"No shadow?" Lucas growled as he unsheathed a sword.

"Clearly not," I replied, searching the skies for the approach of its dark mists.

Tourists started running toward us—they'd obviously been at the tower, or on their way there, and chose the Champ de

Mars as their escape route. Many of them were crying and screaming, their faces panic-stricken as the ghouls zipped after them. The creatures matched the high-pitched notes of the human screams, but theirs were ones of joy—their bony clawed fingers outstretched, rows of shark-like teeth bared while saliva fell from their lips in anticipation.

"Spread out!" Vivienne cried. "Keep looking for the shadow—it can't be far behind."

I crashed my sword into the first ghoul, my blade hitting its skull and splitting the creature's head in two. I needed a full decapitation or dismemberment to kill the creature, so while it was struggling to remove itself from the end of my sword, I cut its neck with a smaller dagger. Its bony body fell to the floor.

Lawrence and I started working together, one of us jabbing the nearest ghoul like a shish-kebab while the other lopped off one of its body parts. We were getting into quite a good routine when Lucas shouted out.

"What the hell?" he yelled. Still keeping my main focus on the ghouls that kept swarming toward us, I quickly glanced to where Lucas was looking. His gaze was fixed on the tower.

I heard a horrific noise, the sound of steel groaning and creaking, so loud it seemed to ricochet off the buildings in the distance and bounce back to my eardrums.

"What *is* that?"

"The ghoul queen," Lucas shouted at us, "she's, uh… grown

since I last saw her."

What?

Finally catching a break with the ghoul onslaught, I looked up at the tower. A ginormous, overweight ghoul was lumbering past the tower, its structure groaning where she'd pushed it aside to reach her prey: *us*.

"You never mentioned her size!" Vivienne yelled, having not heard Lucas.

"She wasn't this big before!" he cried back.

What the… How did she even do that?

She stomped toward us—apparently too heavy to float—her feet shaking the ground with every step. She looked like she was capable of crushing entire buildings, let alone us.

"We need to keep her contained!" I cried. If the ghoul queen got out of the park, Paris would be completely destroyed in a matter of hours. We were talking a Godzilla-like catastrophe.

"I'll do what I can…I'll see if I can shrink her, if not – I might need the sentries for this one," Shayla replied, beckoning to the ministers and ordering them to get barrier-building. We were going to need something sharpish—the ghoul queen was gaining on us, and with the weight and height she was carrying, anything flimsy would be torn apart in a matter of seconds.

Barriers popped up trying to block her way, but she just brushed them aside, roaring down at us in fury.

"It's not working!" Shayla cried. "She's not getting any

smaller – everything I'm sending her way just seems to bounce off."

"Anyone got any other ideas?" Vivienne yelled.

I racked my brains, trying to think of a weak spot or something that we could use as leverage. The deadliest thing about her was her size. Our weapons were useless when faced with such a huge mass—we'd practically need a battering ram to slow her down…

"Wait! We're standing in front of the French military school!" I yelled, spinning around. Sure enough, the vast complex lay in the distance, its grand building hopefully containing thousands of well-trained French soldiers and an arsenal of effective weapons—less medieval joust, more sniper rifles and missile launchers.

"You're a genius!" Shayla burst out.

"Good plan," agreed Vivienne. "Shayla? Can you get us there?"

The ghoul queen was now racing toward us, the ground feeling like it was going to split under her weight.

"I'm all for it—but we're going to need a distraction!" Lucas roared, swiping low to hack off the lower appendages of an approaching ghoul.

"The sentries are going to need to take over," Vivienne replied calmly. She called over to one of the guards nearest to her. The ghoul queen leaned down, her fleshy hands about the same size as a small car, and tried to pick us up from the ground. We narrowly dodged them, my sword almost completely ineffectual. It probably felt like a splinter to her.

The guard and Vivienne battled side by side as she laid out the plan. The guard smiled, looking impressed, and then nodded, backing up to relay the information to the rest of the army. So far we were in luck; the ghoul queen seemed completely preoccupied with us, and less interested in storming through the streets of Paris.

"Now, Shayla!" Vivienne called.

A second later, we were all standing in front of the military building, its large columns and elegant classical architecture making it look more like a palace than anything associated with the military.

"So what's the plan?" Lucas asked. "We just storm in and demand weapons?"

Vivienne looked behind us at the mass of ghouls and the irritated-looking queen.

"Yep, I think we do."

We entered through the main doors, already open, with glamorously-attired officers flooding into the courtyard, all staring in amazement at the nightmare vision of the queen ghoul.

"*Mon Dieu*," the officer closest to me whispered, "*c'est hideux!*" The blood drained from his face and he tried to loosen his starched white collar in agitation.

Vivienne quickly took charge. She approached the most decorated officer, a man who must have been in his seventies, and reeled off impeccable French. The man looked flustered, but ushered us all inside. He quickly led us through the huge galleries and rooms, yelling out instructions to the younger-looking officers who hurried by. Some of them couldn't have been older than eighteen.

He came to a stop in front of a plain-looking door, which looked out of place in the rococo rooms we'd passed, the ceilings hanging with golden chandeliers, gilt wallpaper and huge oil paintings depicting all the battles of France right back to the Napoleonic wars.

With shaking hands, he retrieved a large bunch of keys and proceeded to click, twist and turn the multiple locks on the door. Once it was open, another door stood behind it, reinforced steel with a keypad in the center. Furtively looking around to make sure we weren't watching, he entered a code and the door released, sliding sideways.

"Wow," Xavier breathed.

We all stared in stunned silence.

Forget what the palace of Nevertide provided—*this* was an armory.

"Don't stop and admire," Vivienne snapped, "get anything large enough to take her down—and *hurry*."

Without needing more encouragement, we all rushed into the room at once. The officer looked mildly panicked at our enthusiasm, and even more so when Lucas and Lawrence both approached a table of hand-held missile launchers.

"This looks about right." Lucas smiled.

There were five on the table, each held secure by locks, and a glass case over them which I imagined was fitted with an alarm.

Vivienne gestured to the officer, who hurried to unlock the equipment. I was half amazed that we were given such easy access, but we could already hear the tremors of the queen approaching…time was running out.

"All take one," Vivienne announced when the weapons were freed. "But once we get out there, you fire on my command, not at will. Got it?"

"Got it," we replied—Lucas somewhat sullenly.

"Let's go."

We raced back out of the room, past the halls and palatial surroundings of the school. We arrived at the courtyard with seconds to spare. The ghoul queen was gaining on us—knocking down blue-tinted barriers that the sentries must have tried to put up when they couldn't stop her. She waved them aside like cobwebs.

"*Back!*" Vivienne shouted and gestured at the crowds of French officers. They all backed up hurriedly, creating an opening where we could stand and aim. We stood in a line, each of the weapons pointed at the ghoul. With a steady hand, I rested the butt of the launcher on my shoulder, peering through the sight. I aimed for her neck, presuming that at least in some respects she'd be similar to the rest of her species—only killable by dismemberment.

"Ready!" Vivienne shouted.

I clicked off the safety latch.

"Aim!"

Exhaling slowly, I lined up the aim of the vision cross bar with the tip of the missile.

"Fire!"

Five missiles shot through the air, trailing thin lines of quickly dispersing smoke. They all made their aim—two others hitting the neck along with mine, and one on each shoulder. For a split second nothing happened, then with an ear-splitting boom, the ghoul queen was lit up like a firework display. She screamed with rage before her cry was abruptly cut short. Black and grayish colored innards decorated the gardens, making horrid squelching sounds as they splattered against the trees and the once-smart buildings that surrounded the gates. The body started to tumble backward. I hoped that all the sentries would have had the good sense to have moved out of the way already...

The ground shook one last time, some of the windows breaking in the school behind us, as the ghoul queen landed on the ground—her body almost taking up the entire length of the

Champ de Mars.

"That was a close one," Lawrence breathed.

"I don't think it's over yet," I replied, hearing the screams of an enraged ghoul army heading our way.

Before we could rush forward and attack, Ibrahim appeared out of nowhere, waving to get the attention of Shayla and the rest of us.

"Jenus—he's in the In-Between—you need to move," the warlock shouted.

"I need to tell the sentries they're in charge," Vivienne called out to Shayla. "Get ready to move us!"

She ran off toward the ministers that we'd left in the gardens, and then a few moments later returned, joining our group as Shayla got ready to move us. Ibrahim had already vanished.

"One down, one to go," I muttered to Lawrence. "So much for our romantic dinner."

Bastien

As we appeared in front of a large structure named the "Royal Festival Hall", I took in our mundane human surroundings and was struck once again by how much my life had changed since I'd met Victoria. For the bulk of my years, I'd known almost nothing about lands beyond The Woodlands, and yet now here I was—a member of GASP who could be called to any end of the human or supernatural worlds at an hour's notice. I'd learnt and seen so much of vastly different cultures in such a short space of time that I felt like a different person, and I guessed in many ways I was.

I didn't have long to muse, and quickly focused on the task at hand. I noted that the weather was gloomy and grey, with no direct sunlight, which meant that the vampires could manage without shade. I glanced back to see Claudia and her daughter, safe behind me, her hand clasped in Ash's. Micah and Kira looked ready for a fight, both of them casting their gaze across the river in anticipation. I could sense that the danger was already upon us. Families and groups of students were running alongside the embankment, pushing and shoving their way forward.

"Waterloo" bridge was covered in the dark, sprawling mass of the shadow. I could hear cars screeching and crashing into one another. A large truck, whose driver must have accelerated blindly through the shadow, spun out of control and went crashing down into the "Thames".

Amid the mayhem, I turned to the group behind me.

"This is going to be a damage-limitation mission. We save as many as we can. The shadow is just going to keep coming until we find the entity, so focus on saving lives as much as battling his forces—understood?" They all agreed. The sentries looked slightly skeptical about my strategy, but I figured that human lives weren't that high on their priority list. That was tough, because they were high on mine.

"Arwen, Eli, can you both get in the water and see about that truck driver?" I asked. Without a moment's hesitation, they both started running toward the river. "Micah, Kira, I'm worried about the boats," I continued, watching the tourist guide boats coming to a halt in the river. Their slow-moving engines were trying to pull back and turn around, but the river was starting to resemble a traffic jam. "The rest of us need to get up on that bridge."

Yuri, Ash, Ruby, Claudia and I fought our way through the crowds, jumping up the steps that would lead us to the bridge. When we got there, the road was packed with abandoned cars. Flashing vehicles—ambulance and police—were trying to get through, but most of the medics had run on too, realizing that all the potential victims had run on ahead, surrounding the large movie theater and bringing more of the traffic to a standstill.

The shadow crept toward us slowly, its tentacles of mist wrapping around each of the cars and feeling inside the windows and open doors, hoping to claim human lives.

I jumped up on the back of a car, and heard the others doing the same. Using them as stepping-stones, I ran forward, swords at the ready.

We attacked the shadow as best we could—Yuri using abandoned cars as weapons to hurl at the mists, giving us a few moments' respite between each fresh wave of the enemy's onslaught.

I glanced over the side of the bridge. Micah, Kira and the rest of my group were all hunched low on the rooftops of the boats, waiting to leap to defend the humans below. Most of the tourists and locals recognized us as GASP. For once I was glad of our fame—it meant that we didn't have to worry about terrifying civilians while trying to protect them.

We continued to slice through the shadow army, but before long the mists had started to seep over the sides of the bridge, looking for easier prey.

They weren't going to find it.

The werewolves tensed, watching the shadow's approach. The humans started screaming, no doubt feeling the dark, oppressive dread that the armies could inflict.

Arwen and Eli were dragging the truck driver from the water, making their way to a small emergency boat that was zipping around below the bridge. The emergency team helped the driver climb aboard, and embraced Eli and Arwen, trying to get them to step into heat-retaining blankets.

"Build a barrier!" I called to the sentries behind us. "Make sure it doesn't get any further inland."

If we could isolate them here, saving the humans who were gathered by the massive movie theater, and fight our battle on the boats, we'd have a larger chance of success. The ministers and the guards leapt into action, using the tall buildings to stretch the barrier over one end of the bridge.

Yuri and I jumped off the railings, both landing on a tourist boat beside Micah. A second later, Arwen had helped Claudia, Ash and Ruby to do the same from the emergency boat, sending them flying through the air to join Kira.

The shadow was quick to surround us. I abandoned my swords, finding it easier to rip and tear with my hands. Soon we had quite an audience. The humans below us yelled out helpful tips like, "Behind you!" and, "Yeah—get 'em! Get 'em!" I rolled my eyes at Yuri. Somehow our battle had turned into a spectator sport—but at least the crowds were no longer screaming in horror.

"I hope they hurry up and locate the entity," I called out to Yuri. "This isn't going to stop otherwise."

I looked over to where the sentries were lined up at the end of the bridge. Their barrier was holding up well—the shadow had mostly merged down into the water—but there weren't enough of us to hold it at bay forever.

"We need to evacuate these people!" I called to Arwen, hoping she could hear me. A moment later I heard the emergency boat pull up alongside the bigger tourist yacht.

"What can I do, Bastien?" Arwen asked, sending out spells toward the shadow while she spoke. The mists leapt back momentarily, but didn't let up on their assault.

"We need to get the people out of the boats. If we get called to another location because of the entity, all these people are going to be left defenseless."

"I'll think of something," the witch replied. "Cover me, Eli?"

Eli, who was positioned nearby, nodded, moving at the speed of light to make sure that the younger witch was protected.

She took over from the driver, speeding the little boat out into the middle of the river. There, she cut the engine. She rushed to the side, her hands stretched out over the water.

I continued to fight off the shadow, but kept one eye on the witch. The river water, previously fairly still, was now growing choppier by the second. It was rocking our boat and some of the others, sending the werewolves skittering around the covers of the yachts, unable to get a good grip.

"Careful, Arwen," I warned under my breath, knowing that she wouldn't be able to hear me.

The waters started to rear up. The witch was creating a whirlpool, its force so strong it was practically starting to drain the riverbed. The boats knocked against one another, juddering on impact. But it was working. The mists were getting drawn into the water. A typhoon-type spiral reared upward, slowly becoming level with the skyscrapers in the distance. It sucked in more of the shadow till the waters became as black as night— the howls of the soldiers could be heard emanating from the mists. It wasn't destroying them, but it was holding them at bay.

The spectators from the boats started to whistle and cheer. The mists that surrounded us and the werewolves were drawn away. Eventually, Yuri dropped his swords—there was nothing left to fight.

My only concern now was how long the witch could hold her elemental control.

"Dad!" Arwen cried out, as the warlock appeared in the emergency boat next to her. She didn't break her hold over the water, but grinned broadly as her father looked up at the whirlpool in amazement and gave her a nod of approval.

"I need to take you to the In-Between," Ibrahim called out. "The rest are already there. We found Jenus."

Finally.

We jumped boats, moving closer to the warlock.

"Are you going to be okay on your own?" I asked Arwen, worried about leaving the young witch in control.

"Yeah, it's fine. I've got the sentries as well," she added, glancing up to the bridge.

"Okay," I replied, squeezing the girl's arm in gratitude.

I turned to Ibrahim.

"We're ready."

SHERUS

It was good to be home. The moment we exited the swirling portal walls and stepped out into the peaceful expanse of the In-Between, my heart leapt. The great void of stars and eternal night was just as it should have been—I could see the planets of the fae glowing brightly in the distance, and the red hue of my own home beckoning to me. As much as I feared what might be following us—or might have already arrived—I couldn't help but feel a certain amount of pride to be welcoming Queen Nuriya to my home. I wanted her to witness the splendor of the fae—the beauty of my planet with its red rivers, its glowing stones that matched the colors of her eyes.

"Not long now, brother." Lidera smiled at me as we

transported the rest of the team toward the fire planet. The sentries muttered at the back of the line, all fearful of the wide expanse of space, but they had enough sense not to break the chain. I had to admit, the deafening silence still took some getting used to.

I sped up our passage, and a few moments later we were standing in the courtyard of my palace, the ice fires dancing merrily from their fountains and a few soldiers and guards going about their business as usual. As they saw us, each and every one of them bent low in greeting.

"I think we might've pre-empted the arrival of the shadow," Ben murmured to me as I ushered my subjects to rise. I agreed— certainly there didn't seem to be anything amiss here.

"Let's not be too hasty," Queen Nuriya added. "Something doesn't feel right—it's *too* quiet."

She was right. It felt like the kingdom had taken a collective inhale of breath—that the entire planet was in mid-motion, paused as it waited for something to happen.

The danger came so quietly and calmly, we were in the thick of it before I had time to realize what had actually happened.

One moment I was looking around, trying to put my finger on the source of the disease, the next Jenus ambled toward us from the doors of the palace, a smile across his face, his posture relaxed and open, as if he were greeting old friends.

"Stand back!" Ben ordered.

We froze, waiting to see what Jenus would do next. For once the wretched creature was clean, and elaborately dressed in fae clothing. He must have been here for a while, making himself at home in my chambers. Why had no one stopped him? Guards were ambling about everywhere, but they almost seemed completely oblivious to him.

"What have you done to them?" I growled.

Nothing, king of fae. I informed them we were old friends—I can be very persuasive, you know.

I felt sickened. He'd obviously manipulated my men into letting him in the palace. I couldn't imagine what kind of devastation he would have left in his wake within the walls of my home.

"Airos is in there," Lidera gasped, referring to her favored man-servant. She went to move forward but I held her back. She struggled in my arms, tears pouring down her face. I didn't let go. I could practically *smell* death leaking out of the doors behind Jenus.

Jenus watched us struggle, smiling to himself.

"Ibrahim, you know what to do," Ben murmured to the warlock. A moment later the man vanished—on his way to fetch the others. I hoped that he would return in time. Jenus was like a cobra, his deadly calm evidence of the vicious strike that would shortly follow.

"Why here?" I asked, unable to help myself. "Why are you so

bent on destroying the land of the fae? What is it to you?"

It was this aspect of the entity that puzzled me most. A creature who had resided in Nevertide since the dawn of time, fixated on the In-Between—it was strange. How had the two dimensions ever collided? I had never heard of Nevertide until recently, and its distance from our lands made it seem illogical that the entity would choose this as the location to wreak its revenge.

Nothing but your arrogance, mighty Sherus. The fae have long believed themselves the superiors of all other supernatural beings— you trick and manipulate, you squabble among yourselves over the immense riches of your planets combined. It is your home that I choose as my seat of power, your home where the greatest of the fae bounty lies in your precious stones of fire, your home where my children will once again grow and prosper, annihilating all that would stand in our way.

I fell silent at his words, and Lidera stopped her struggling.

"It's not true," she whispered pitifully.

But it had been.

Perhaps not now, with our less than easy alliance with the other planets, but I knew the reputation the fae had within some of the other dimensions. That we had managed to garner such hatred from one species—whatever the entity and its shadow was—surprised me. But perhaps it shouldn't have.

"You are hardly one to cast judgment on us," I spat out.

I don't pretend to be your moral superior—I just wish to destroy you.

Jenus grinned.

"Guards!" I called out to the fae armies. "Seize him!"

They rushed toward him, spears held aloft and their armor gleaming. Jenus knocked them away like insects, sending them sprawling backwards with a slight move of his hands, like they were a minor inconvenience.

"Sherus," Ben warned me. "Don't send more of your men to die. We need to wait till the others arrive—remember; defend not attack."

He repeated what Derek had said to each group before we left Nevertide.

"He's alone," I hissed, "it's our chance."

"No—I don't think he is. Can't you feel it?" Ben replied, looking anxiously up into the clear skies. There wasn't a cloud in sight—the only feeling I was experiencing was rage, directed at the repugnant creature standing at the doors of my home as if he already owned it.

"No," I replied firmly. "His arrogance has clearly gotten the better of him. If he thinks he can defeat us all single-handedly, then let us give him that opportunity!"

"You are too hasty!" Lidera cried. "Ben's right. I *can* feel something—and so can she."

Lidera pointed at Queen Nuriya. She was standing some way

off from us, her face the whitest I'd ever seen it and her large, almond-shaped eyes fearful. She was looking up into the open sky, her eyes seeming to see beyond the hues of the planet's atmosphere into the black abyss we'd just come from.

"The planet of the stones," she whispered, her voice dry. "It has awoken."

The soft blue of the sky ruptured violently. The shadow army broke through the barriers that had been set up around our planet and started to spill out over our heads, casting the light in an inky black.

Queen Nuriya was right, the shadow was larger than I believed possible. The stones must have cracked as the ones in Nevertide had, releasing an army which would contain millions—not thousands.

What say you now, king of the fire fae? Will you beg for my mercy before the day is done, or will you die like the rest of your kind, believing till the last breath is ripped out of you that you could defeat me?

"Prepare for battle," Ben commanded, ignoring the voice of the entity. "Focus on Jenus, not the shadow. When he dies, the rest will follow."

I drew my sword, yelling for the armies of the fae to assemble.

TEJUS

As soon as we landed on the planet of the fae, with Corrine's help, we were immediately thrust into the mayhem of the battle. There was no time to be terrified at the sheer size of the shadow that had descended on the land. I swung the sword of Hellswan in every direction, each time making contact with the ashen armies.

"Hazel, stay with me!" I shouted to her, making sure that we were battling side by side. What *did* almost petrify me was the lack of any location that could be considered 'safe' or at least out of harm's way. If things got difficult, there would be nowhere for Hazel to escape to. The shadow was everywhere.

Dragging Hazel with me, I saw the figure of Ben ahead. He

was thrashing wildly at the mists. His roar of rage seemed to drown out everything else. Ash and Ruby followed behind us, and I was glad to see them there. It felt right that if this was the last battle with the entity and its armies—as I hoped that it would be—I would be fighting beside my emperor—the only one of us, really, who had cared about whether or not Nevertide survived. I owed him loyalty, and the protection of my sword.

"Tejus," Ben called out, seeing us approach. "We need to get you to Jenus. Last I saw of him was by the entrance to the fae castle, but he was swallowed up by the mists. Do you think you can call on your brother?"

"That's what I'm hoping," I replied. "Where's the entrance?"

Ben gestured straight ahead, and all five of us moved through the mists, each defending our small unit as best we could.

"This is impossible," Ash raged, "how are there so many of them?"

"We think the planet of the stones erupted in the In-Between, much like they did in Nevertide," Ben called out. "What about the barrels of the immortal water? Can they do something?"

"The witches are dealing with it. Hopefully we'll see some results soon," Ash replied, charging on, his sword swinging into the darkness.

Tejus of Hellswan, came a voice. We couldn't see the entity, but clearly it could see us. *I deduce from the presence of these armies that your brother has been abusing his power. However, I can't say*

I'm disappointed to see you here—you and your emperor can witness the destruction of fae lands, and can perhaps commiserate with them, your own land as unfit for purpose as theirs.

The shadow started to move back, revealing the stone steps that led up to Sherus's palace. Standing at their apex was Jenus— clean shaven, his hair neatly tied back, and wearing the richly embroidered gowns of the fae. He held no weapons, but as he raised his arms up, further separating the mists like a curtain, there was no doubt about who had the superior power. An entire army of millions at his disposal.

His face rested in a sly smile, his eyes slowly taking in the group. There was no evidence of panic or fear, just a knowing look saying that we would fail, that he was undefeatable. I didn't know if it was because the monster wore the face of my brother, or because I felt that Jenus *was* the monster, but I lost my head and launched at him with a cry, every fiber of my being wanting to destroy him, eradicate him from this dimension and all the others.

I played right into his hands.

Laughing, Jenus swatted me away, sending me flying into Ash, putting us both at risk from the encroaching shadow. We scrambled to our feet. The shadow moved back further, allowing us a pool of light. I wondered why the entity had called back its armies from attacking us, when I could hear the fighting continuing elsewhere. Jenus stepped into the space, and the armies followed him. We were completely surrounded—cut off from the entrance to the palace that I'd envisioned being our only possible escape option.

The smirking face of my brother was making my blood boil.

"Tejus," Hazel gripped my arm and whispered, "call him."

I nodded, waiting for the right moment. I glanced over at Ash, who gave me the briefest of nods and launched himself at Jenus. Ben followed him, both warriors battling the entity best they could.

While he was distracted, I tried to call out to my brother. I let my mind wander across the confined space, letting Jenus know that I was there. I drifted past Ash, feeling his anger and rage at the creature, but also his pride, how he wouldn't let himself be defeated at the hands of the entity once again. I drifted past Ruby, sensing her fear and determination, the worry she had for her parents, but most of all Ash. Ben's energy was bright, purer than the rest of us, a brilliant flame that was only preoccupied with justice—with bringing down the creature, with forbidding him to take the land of the fae, that land Ben felt he was partly bound to. Hazel's energy I didn't need to feel with my mind. I knew what it would contain. I knew her fear and anger were intertwined, but that her hope would overshadow both those emotions, trusting that we could end the entity somehow, that we could perhaps even bring back a repentant Jenus from the dead.

I loved her for that hope, but I felt it was misplaced.

I reached toward Jenus, feeling nothing but a sickening darkness, a bleak despair that I'd never known, so wretched and absent of any light that everything about it felt gray and dead, as if the mind wasn't even alive. I kept trying, mentally prodding the creature as he tried to destroy Ash and Ben.

A few moments later, just at the point in which I was going to give up on the idea and join in the fight, I felt a flicker of anger—a small, twisted whisper of jealousy and hate, emanating from the figure of Jenus. I latched onto it, feeling it with my mind, recognizing the feelings as those belonging to my brother, not the creature who borrowed his form. As our energy met, the emotions changed to relief and recognition, and I could *feel* Jenus, the imperfect brother of mine who had gotten it so horribly wrong—whose pride, hatred and acid jealousy had been his own downfall. The same brother who reached out for me now, begging for forgiveness.

I held the energy, bringing it forward, chasing his mind with my own. I hesitated for the briefest moment before latching on to Hazel's hand. Our three minds met, the energy electrifying. A border sprang up, pure and white, appearing as a great flame engulfing us all. Ben, who had been knocked back by the entity only a split second before, was blown back by the force, flung into the shadow, and Hazel screamed out his name.

I held her tightly, not letting her cross the barriers of white light to reach her uncle. She fought me, but my grip didn't falter.

The angrier she became, the more desperate as she heard Ben's roars of fury as he battled the ashen army, the higher the flames rose. Before long, not a sound could be heard other than the screams of the entity. They were so loud, it was as if they were coming from every single creature that had broken out of the stones—one cry becoming a million.

The fires were burning the entity, their purity washing out its darkness, blazing against the blackness of its soul.

Jenus's face became a contorted mask of pain, and he reached for the barriers, desperate to get out. They would not let him pass. The flames leapt onto his robe and hair, snaking their way up his body. He turned his anger toward us, his flaming body ready to pounce. Before he could move, he let out one last scream, a torrent of black tar vomiting from his mouth. It didn't fall to the floor, instead, like it was a live, conscious *thing*, it started to circle the wall of flames.

I shoved Hazel behind me; the ichorous black liquid narrowly missed her, and instead shot into Ash's open mouth, filling up his nostrils and eye sockets—consuming the emperor of Nevertide.

BENEDICT

Yelena and I were being held by Sky again, zooming over the Dauoa forest and beyond into the wasteland of Nevertide.

"Blue and Rock are up ahead," Sky pointed out. We watched as the Hawks flew closer. They must have been on their way back to find us. I hoped they had good news. Sky stopped, hovering in the air by flapping his wings rapidly.

"What are you doing?" Blue asked. "We need to keep looking for the jinni. We're running out of time. The others have left already!"

"We found her! But what do you mean they *left*?" I shouted.

"The entity left the portal, with its armies. What do you mean *her*?" Rock replied, equally baffled.

"Long story. Let's get down to the cove."

They left?

How did they think they were going to battle the entity in the other dimensions if they couldn't manage to defeat him here? They didn't even know that the shadow was actually made up of super-ghouls; information like that might have made a big difference.

We carried on our journey, Sky moving as swiftly as he could with Julian, Fly, and Ridan behind us.

A short while later, we landed on the shore. Horatio, Aisha and the Oracle were waiting for us, staring at the portal. The rest of the place looked deserted.

"We missed them—you must have known!" I stormed up to the Oracle, furious that we'd missed our chance.

She turned to me, her barely-there blue eyes staring down at me, but seeming to look past me, as if I wasn't really there. It was freaky when she did that, and annoying.

"I told you we were too late," she sighed.

I groaned in frustration. Trying to pull myself together, I bit out, "How are they going to win this if they can't get the entity back in the stones? You must have known this was going to happen. Why didn't you leave your stupid cave earlier? Why didn't you come and find *us*?"

Julian and Yelena were both glaring up at her too, all of us waiting for an answer that would change our minds about burying her in the sand and leaving her to rot. I looked around for Horatio and Aisha, but they were just standing in front of the water, looking worried.

"Be patient." She smiled. "There is another way—all is not lost. The leaders of Nevertide—brave sentries—are making choices right now that will lead to happier times…new beginnings and regeneration."

"That means literally *nothing*," I replied angrily. "Tell me what's going to happen to my family—to the entity."

"That I can't see," she sighed in her whimsical way. "There are too many unknowns. I am sorry, young soldier, I can give you no more than that."

I turned away in disgust. What was the point of an Oracle if they couldn't even answer the simplest question?

"I think I can see Zerus and Field," Julian commented, looking toward the far edge of the cove. I followed his gaze, watching as the Hellswan sentry stepped into view. I was surprised that they hadn't taken him with them, but I supposed he was a bit too out of it to be much help in a fight.

"I thought I recognized you," he muttered as he approached. "There are other villagers hiding along the cliff edge. They are waiting to be told whether or not to leave this land."

I looked past him, now noticing villagers starting to emerge from the wild shrubbery that grew on the opposite side of the cove – Queen Memenion with them.

"Did you tell Tejus everything?" I asked Zerus.

"I did. My brother seems different now," he mused.

"Which one?"

"Tejus," he replied, looking at me like I was an idiot. "He is different. Kinder, perhaps. More in control of his temper and his rage...I wonder if in the past I judged him too harshly."

I shrugged. I wasn't that concerned with Zerus's thoughts on his brother—more with whether or not Tejus was going to survive the battle, and my sister and family along with him.

"Have you heard anything from Jenus?" I pressed.

"No." The sentry shook his head. "He has been silent, I'm afraid."

"I'm going to see if Jenney's with the villagers," Julian said, walking away from us with his shoulders hunched. Not knowing what else to do, I ran after my friend, Yelena joining us.

"Julian, wait!" I called out.

He stopped, his brown eyes despondent.

"What?" he asked.

"I don't think we should give up hope," I said. "I know the Oracle's talking nonsense, but new beginnings sound good, right? I mean, she's not saying we're doomed or anything."

"No," Julian replied slowly, "but new beginnings can mean a lot of things. Not necessarily good. We're standing in what's basically a wasteland while everyone goes off to fight—despite the fact that the last battle failed. Has it occurred to you what will happen if GASP fails this time? If the entity gets back here before they do, or the shadow? We'll all be dead. And in the meantime, we have nothing to do but wait, *once again.*"

Julian had a point.

I slumped down onto the sand, suddenly feeling dejected.

"Do you think we should go after them?" I asked. "We can probably get to Earth—maybe Aisha will take us to where the battle's happening?"

"I don't think that's a great idea," Julian replied, kicking a stone.

"Then we can only do the next right thing," Yelena replied, her hands on her hips. "If we're the last to stand against the entity, then we need to make sure we're ready. There's a bunch of old Viking weapons over by the water. There's the three of us, Zerus, two powerful jinn and the only creature in the entire universe that's defeated the entity in the past! Why are you being such wimps? We have an army!"

"Not to mention the villagers," I added, my mind coming alive at her speech. Some of them were pretty fierce.

"Exactly!" Yelena cried.

Okay. This was good. I looked over at Julian, who smiled reluctantly.

"Let's get some weapons then," he agreed.

If the battle was going to come to us, we'd be ready.

Ash

The black tar-like liquid flew around the barrier. I raised my sword, hoping to cut it down in its tracks, but as I cried out to Ruby, telling her to stand back, the tar slid past my blade. The last thing I saw was a black emptiness shooting toward my face—too fast for me to do anything other than cry out.

I felt it enter me. Its cold thickness slid down my throat, drowning me, filling my lungs as on reflex I inhaled it urgently, desperate for air. It blinded me, my eyes wide open in horror but seeing a void of nothingness—as if the very *thing* that was attacking me was nothing.

The liquid flooded through my body, reaching every vein and nerve, restricting all my senses. From a distance, I could hear the screams of Ruby and Hazel, the bellow of rage from Tejus, but none of it seemed to matter. Their pain and shock were happening far, far away—too many dimensions away to mean anything to me.

Welcome me.

The voice purred inside me, its whisper curling inside my organs. I felt omnipotent, glimpsing a sense of power inside me that far outweighed anything I'd ever thought possible. I also felt a flicker of desire that was mine—reaching out for the entity, wanting it to take me, to show me a future where there was no pain, no death—just eternity and the infinite possibilities of every single species trembling in my presence.

"Don't—Ash—don't!"

I heard Ruby crying. It was still an abstract sound, something I could have dismissed like all the other voices of my friends, but there was something in the tone—the hitched cry, the desperation that it held—which reminded me of things that I sensed the entity wanted me to forget.

"You've got to fight it! Don't leave me—you said that we weren't done yet—you *promised!*"

The flicker of desire that had leapt up in me in response to the entity's power was still there, but it had dimmed. I was reminded of Ruby, the girl I'd pulled from a cellar, whose bright blue eyes had glared at me in mistrust. Just one look at her had made me think that she was the most *alive* thing I'd ever witnessed. I remembered the night in the summer palace, the way her skin glowed, her voice, her soft laughter and the burning marks she'd left on my skin where she touched me.

I wanted that warmth, not this darkness.

I can give you eternity, the entity whispered, *immortality, lifetimes of glory.*

A lot of people had been offering me immortality lately. The Impartial Ministers, Ruby's mother, and now the entity. I wasn't interested. Not if there wasn't Ruby to share it with.

The moment my decision was made, a searing pain splintered through my body, as if I was tearing apart from the inside. My body stopped belonging to me. Fires felt like they were consuming my blood, my soul separating from its home as it rejected the insurmountable pain. Was this what dying felt like?

The entity screamed; my fire was its fire, my pain its pain.

I didn't know how long the torture lasted. Every second felt like a year. I believed the pain would never stop, that immortality *had* been given, and that this was what it would feel like till the end of time, the fires unrelenting, my silent screams never being heard.

"He's moving," Ruby breathed.

It was the first coherent noise that I'd heard since the pain began. As her voice floated over to me, the burning sensation slowly started to recede. My body was able to experience the fresh coolness of air on my skin, my veins feeling like they'd been cleansed somehow—of tar, of fire, of the entity.

I tried to open my eyes, praying that the abyss would no longer be there, that I would be able to see the blonde halo of hair and blue eyes that had saved me. Again.

My eyelids flickered open, feeling like heavy weights. I didn't see the blue of Ruby's eyes—instead I saw the blue of a bright sky, not as beautiful but rewarding all the same. A second later, Ruby peered down at me.

"Ash?"

"Hey, Shortie," I rasped, the words feeling unfamiliar on my tongue.

"That's the second time you've almost died on me. Can you stop doing that?" she barked, her expression furious.

"Yeah." I smiled. There she was. My livewire, my future wife who didn't just shine brightly, she was practically a forest fire.

Hands grabbed me. It was Tejus and Ruby, helping me to sit up. I looked around at their faces—a mixture of awestruck dumbness and worry. The barrier of fire had disappeared, and the shadow had changed too. It was no longer a dark mass, but thousands and thousands of soldiers in their ashen form, fighting with the fae army, GASP and the sentry ministers and guards.

I wondered why they hadn't come toward us.

"There's a barrier up," Tejus replied helpfully, "a regular one. What happened?"

His tone was brusque, but his eyes betrayed relief and joy—intense emotions that I'd not seen him display unless he was looking at Hazel.

"I don't exactly know," I murmured. "I think the entity chose the wrong body...I felt the immortal waters, like fire running through me—I think they might have *purged* him somehow."

I didn't mention the choice I'd made to activate them. How close a call it had been. Part of me had welcomed the entity—its offer had been tempting. If it wasn't for Ruby, it wouldn't have ended the same way.

"What's happened to the shadow?" I asked.

Tejus eyed me speculatively, but turned to watch the battle taking place around us. We were winning, easily. Ben took out six of the soldiers in one swipe of his sword. I was glad he was still alive.

"As soon as you shone white, the shadow changed, leaving only the soldiers," Tejus replied matter-of-factly.

What?

"I shone white?"

"You looked like you were on fire," Ruby muttered. "Like, your whole body—as if you were part of the barrier."

Splatters of water started to rain down on us. I looked up to the sky, puzzled.

"There." Tejus nodded his head over to where a group of witches were standing—Ibrahim, Mona and Corrine were manipulating the immortal water that had been brought along in barrels. It rained down on the ashen soldiers, burning them.

"We should help." I tried to stand up, but Ruby held me down.

"Do you know what? I think you've done enough today. You can rest and leave this to the others." Her tone warned me not to argue with her. Somehow, despite presumably being the hero of the hour, I was in deep trouble.

"Fine," I agreed, yanking her down next to me. If I wasn't fighting, neither was she.

"You too, Hazel, Tejus," Ruby bit out at our friends. "You can all just sit right here. I've had enough of you all being in danger—we've done what we can, so we can just wait it out now, okay?"

Tejus smirked at her, but did as she asked. Hazel sat down too, and we sat in silence, watching GASP and the rest of the sentries get to work. It was like watching some kind of orchestrated dance performance—the vampires, fae armies and Sherus, werewolves, witches, dragons and Hawks were so elegant in their slaughter.

"Impressive," Tejus breathed. I could see he was itching to get out and join them. Hazel took his hand, stilling him. Words, unspoken, passed between them and he nodded, pulling her into his arms.

This final battle wasn't ours.

Hazel

When there were only a few of the entity's soldiers left, Tejus took down the barriers. Ruby and Tejus helped Ash to his feet, and we looked around at the weary GASP members and sentries. The only ones who didn't look like they were half-dead on their feet were the fae armies—they had been battling the shortest amount of time, and still looked pristine in their elaborate uniforms.

I looked around for my parents and saw them standing by an autumn-leaved tree, helping the wounded. They were safe and unharmed. My mom was attending to Micah, who had a cut running along his side. It didn't look too serious though, and Mona was approaching—I had every faith that she'd patch him up in no time.

"How are you feeling, Ash?" I asked.

"Okay," he replied. "Been better, been worse."

Ruby and I smiled at each other, but her eyes seemed dulled—the smile more of an act than anything genuine. She'd been through a lot. Having Ash almost dying twice was more than any sane person could bear, and I could understand that she wasn't exactly in a celebratory mood. Neither was I. I'd imagined this moment being very different—once the entity was dead we'd all be overjoyed, patting ourselves on the back for making it through and defeating our enemy. It didn't feel that way at *all*. I just felt exhausted—and sad. I thought of all the people who had been lost—Memenion, Varga, the villagers, the Acolytes, Queen Trina, Jenus. Some of them deserved our pity, some didn't. But they had all suffered at the hands of the entity. I thought about Benedict, Julian and Yelena too—how much they had gone through to reach today. It just seemed like a waste of their innocence. It wasn't like any of us would ever forget what had happened. It might have made us all a bit tougher, a bit harder and more resilient. But at what cost?

Tejus turned away from our group, walking over to a body that was slumped on the ground. No one had bothered to approach it, and the limbs sprawled out, lifeless on the ground.

It was Jenus. His eyes stared upward at the sky.

Tejus knelt down and gently closed his eyelids. I joined him, wrapping the fae cloak around Jenus' body. He looked more peaceful than I'd ever seen him in life.

"I should have been a better brother," Tejus muttered.

"So should he," I replied gently. I felt pity for Jenus, but I wouldn't forget how he had tried to use me as his pawn, trying to get me to end Tejus's life in exchange for my brother's. How he'd locked Benedict, Julian and Ruby up when they were meant to be released.

"I'm glad he's at peace. I don't think he experienced much of it while he was alive. I think he was his own worst enemy, not just in the end, but all through his life." Tejus covered his face with the last fold of the cloak.

I nodded. In some ways, Tejus could have been talking about himself.

"You're a good man, you know that—don't you?" I replied.

He turned to me in surprise. He was silent for a moment before replying. "I have reason to try. He didn't."

"As long as you remember that."

Tejus took my hand, turning us both away from the body of his brother. He moved closer to me, his eyes boring down into mine.

"Do you think for a moment that I'd ever forget?" he breathed. "Do you think I don't know that if it wasn't for you, it could easily be me lying in my brother's place?"

"That's not true!"

He smiled.

"It is. And that's okay. I know who I am—I know what I am, and what I'm capable of. But I also know *you*. What you're capable of saving me from."

He kissed me, pulling me closer against him. It was unhurried—slow and lingering, like we had all the time in the world. For the first time since I'd met him, I supposed we did.

* * *

My grandpa interrupted us some time later. He cleared his throat. I untangled myself from Tejus while Grandpa's gaze settled at some point off in the distance till I was standing, flustered and floaty, in front of him.

"GASP members are going to be dispatched to the other locations around Earth to finish off the shadow and the ghouls, but I think that you four should return to Nevertide in the meantime—Benedict and the others will need to be told what's happened, and the villagers too."

"Will you join us back there, after?" I asked.

"We will," he replied. "I think it's still prudent to search for this group of jinn, if they haven't already been found. There are still answers that I want—an assurance that this is the end of it."

I nodded.

Yeah. Answers would be good.

"Queen Nuriya and Corrine will take you back."

"Okay, thanks," I replied.

"No, thank you, Hazel," my grandpa countered. "I couldn't be more proud of you and Benedict if I tried. You have both turned out to be... extremely impressive." He smiled broadly and I fell silent, not really knowing what to say. I felt a flush appearing on my cheeks to see my grandpa so pleased with me, and turned away to tell Ruby and Ash that we'd be leaving.

They were sitting next to one of the fire fountains, both of them staring into space. At first I wondered if they'd had an argument, but they were holding hands. Maybe they were just exhausted.

"We've been asked to head back to Nevertide, tell the others what's happened," I announced. Ruby paled, but stood up with Ash, ready to go.

"If you want to stay..." I hesitated, looking at Ruby. Maybe she'd prefer to stay with her parents or head back to The Shade.

"No," she replied quickly, "It's fine, honestly. I'm just tired."

Ash looked at her, worried.

She smiled that strange, empty smile at him.

"So, who's getting us there?" she asked brightly.

Ash and I looked at each other. Something was up with Ruby, and I knew that it had to do with Ash and the danger he'd just been in, but there was nothing I could say to make her feel any better. We would just have to hope that it wore off in its own time.

"Corrine and Nuriya," I replied.

The witch and the jinni appeared the moment I said their names.

"You know the drill," Corrine muttered, "hold hands."

A second later, we were standing in the star-studded vacuum of the In-Between dimension, traveling slowly away from the planets of the fae. The silence was uncomfortably oppressive, but I clutched Tejus's hand, knowing that it would come to an end soon. Up ahead I saw the bluish, swirling portal that would lead us out onto the snowy peaks of Mount Logan.

We stepped inside the tunnel, the force of the wind knocking into us.

"Stay together!" Corrine called out.

She led us through, the jinni following behind. I glanced over at Tejus, both of our expressions probably matching—crossing through the tunnel was something I'd only ever experienced hours before on the way here, and it was *strange*.

Once we arrived at Mount Logan, Corrine and Nuriya transported us to the North Sea. There we hovered for a few moments over the ocean, while the mouth of the portal became visible. We followed Corrine in, traveling once again through the bluish tunnel that would lead to the cove.

When we arrived in Nevertide, Corrine and Nuriya helped us once again by transporting us to the shore. The sea had become unfrozen, waves gently moving against the sand beds.

"Hazel!"

Benedict was running toward me, his face set in a mixture of disbelief and joy at seeing us all alive.

"Miss me?" I laughed, wrapping his body in my arms.

"Where are Mom and Dad?" he asked, untangling himself a moment later.

"Not far away. They're just finishing up, they'll be here soon."

"And the entity?"

"Dead," I confirmed.

"Really dead?"

"The deadest."

"Awesome," he breathed.

I smiled. That about summed it up.

BENEDICT

I couldn't believe that we'd *won*.

I was so relieved that they were all alive—and not wounded, miraculously—that I completely forgot all about the Oracle, who was still standing back from the shore line.

"Who's your friend?" Ruby asked, glancing over at her.

Then everyone turned and stared.

"It's the Oracle," I replied proudly. She might be as useful as a wet blanket in a storm, but we'd still accomplished our mission and found the person responsible for locking up the entity in the first place.

"What?" Hazel replied, looking at her in confusion.

"It wasn't a group of jinn that locked it up—it was just her.

She's half Ancient, half jinni. Apparently, she's lived in Nevertide since she was little. I'll be honest," I continued in a whisper, "she's kind of…weird. And not a very good Oracle."

"A totally crap Oracle," added Julian, less bothered about keeping his voice down. Then again, she'd probably seen that insult coming.

"I need to have a word with her," said Corrine, looking stunned.

"Be my guest," I replied. She should be answerable to everyone—she'd let us all suffer a lot of bother for no good reason. Just because everything had turned out okay, it didn't mean she should be let off the hook, as far as I was concerned.

Corrine, Nuriya, and the rest of them all started walking toward her. The Oracle looked pleased as they approached – I guessed she could sense them. It struck me that she wasn't very self-aware…maybe that came from living in a cave all by yourself for thousands of years.

I followed with Julian and Yelena.

"Thank you for ending the life of the entity." She smiled at them all before they could get a word in. "Better this way than being re-imprisoned by the stones. Nevertide, and I, are grateful—your names will not be forgotten. You have sacrificed much."

"Yeah, we have," Ruby spat out. "No thanks to you."

"Perhaps," the Oracle mused. "Or perhaps not."

There go those stellar prophecy skills.

"What's that supposed to mean?" Ruby bit back. She was *mad.* I wondered if something had happened in the battle, something that had pissed Ruby off. Ash was alive, and I assumed her parents were otherwise she would have said something, so I couldn't really understand what was bothering her so much—not to this point of fury, anyway. I glanced at Hazel, who shook her head with a 'don't ask' expression.

The Oracle reached out and held Ruby's hand. She looked like she wanted to shake it off but something stopped her.

"Ashbik won't come to further harm, Ruby. You'll have a happy life together, a long life. You two are the new beginning that I spoke of earlier, Tejus of Hellswan and Hazel as well. But it is under your rule that Nevertide will transform—will become truly free."

The Oracle released her hand and stepped back.

"Thank you," Ruby whispered. She wiped at her face hastily, looking as if she was crying.

"I should return to my home," the Oracle added.

"Wait," Nuriya interjected. "I'm afraid you can't do that yet. The rest of GASP will want to question you. I understand that you may have helped us in ways we do not realize, but we need to know the full story, and I would prefer it if you waited for Derek and Sherus to arrive."

"You don't trust me," sighed the Oracle.

"No," Nuriya answered honestly. "I don't. The fact that you're a child of an Ancient and a jinni of old is curious, if not downright terrifying. I hope you understand."

The Oracle fiddled with her dress, looking uncomfortable. "I have told the children and the other jinni my story," she replied softly.

Nuriya crossed her arms.

"That's not enough. Please, you must stay."

"But if I stay now," the Oracle replied, "my own future becomes very unclear."

"They can't harm you," Aisha replied. "It's in the best interest of us all for you to stay a while—yourself included. We need to confirm what you've told us. There's a lot we don't understand about the sentries and their history that you do."

I hid a smirk.

Oh, yeah.

My sister was technically part-ghoul. So gross. I didn't know if I wanted to tell her or wait until she found out from the Oracle…Either way was tempting. Maybe I'd wait for the right moment—let her relax a bit from the battle first. Enjoy her last moments of ignorance before I spilled the beans.

"Are you okay, Benedict?" Yelena asked.

"Yeah!"

"You look like you're choking."

In delight!

"I'm fine," I replied hurriedly.

Yelena gave me a baffled look and then shrugged, turning her attention back to the Oracle.

* * *

The Oracle agreed to stay. She made it clear that she wasn't all that pleased about it, but she stopped resisting. It was strange to come across a creature that was part Ancient, who seemed so compliant – not bent on destroying us all, but almost as if she was afraid of *us* in some ways.

Nuriya and Corrine sent the villagers back to Memenion's castle. Ash would come and see them shortly to give further instructions, and make sure they all had some way of feeding themselves until they could return to their farming. I guessed most of them expected him to go with them, but I got the impression that he didn't want to leave Ruby's side, and none of us were willing to go back into the depths of Nevertide. We all wanted a break, and to get home as soon as we could. Even Zerus stayed with us. He didn't say much to anyone, least of all his brother, but he seemed content enough to just sit still, staring up at the torn sky, waiting for the stars to come out.

Aisha and Horatio lit a massive fire – which Ridan decided to help with—and as the twilight came, we were all sitting around it, using the old Viking remains as stools and chairs. The driftwood made the fire burn strange blue and purple colors, lighting up relaxed and content faces.

The Hawk boys all sat together, poking sticks into the fire and laughing loudly at their own jokes. Ash, Tejus, Ruby and Hazel mostly just looked exhausted, but in a gross, lovey-dovey way. Both pairs snuggled up together, talking in soft whispers. Lucifer, Tejus's haughty lynx, had miraculously appeared from the undergrowth nearby – he'd obviously followed us when we left the castle. I was kind of in awe of the animal…I knew cats were meant to have nine lives, but this one seemed to be completely indestructible. The jinn and Corrine kept passing perfectly cooked corn-type vegetables over to us—they'd managed to do some exploring in the nearby villages and fields before the sun went down to find something edible. It was easily the best food I'd had in months—possibly ever.

The only people who looked less than happy were Yelena and the Oracle.

"Don't you like corn?" I asked Yelena, nudging her. She had been looking at her smoked husk for ages and not taken a single bite.

"I do." She sighed. "But do you want mine? I'm not hungry."

"Yeah," I replied happily, taking it.

"Benedict," Aisha called to me, "Yelena is *upset.*"

"Because she's not *hungry*," I explained.

"No," the jinni snapped, "she's not hungry *because* she's upset. Goodness, child—you are something else." She flung her hands up in the air, turning back to Horatio.

"Are you?" I asked, looking at Yelena.

"I don't know." She shrugged. "It's just that…I guess it's all over now. I have to return home—and there's going to be no more adventures, no more Nevertide, no more *nothing*. I'm going to miss the sentries."

"Really?" I asked, surprised. "You're going to miss the sentries?"

"Well—yeah. Jenney, Ash, Tejus. Won't you?"

I hadn't really thought about it. I was just glad it was all over, and I certainly wouldn't be missing Nevertide.

"I don't *want* to go home," she added fiercely.

"Yelena," Fly interrupted gently. "It's good that you've got a home to go to. Won't your parents be missing you?"

"I guess," she muttered. "Maybe."

"I think they probably will," Sky added. "You're easily missable—trust me, they'll be wanting you home."

Yelena smiled a small smile.

"Thanks," she replied, blushing.

"You can come and visit The Shade whenever you like," I replied, a bit annoyed that the Hawks were saying all the stuff *I* was supposed to be saying. She was my friend, not theirs.

"Really?" she asked, her face brightening.

"Yeah. My mom loves you. She'll like it if you came to stay."

She smiled.

"Can I have my corn back?" she asked. "I'm starving."

ROSE

We returned to Nevertide. The moment we stepped out of the portal I scoured the land for Benedict and Hazel. I saw them, black forms all sleeping around a long-dead fire. I had almost forgotten it was the middle of the night.

"Should we wake them?" Claudia asked.

Behind me, coming out of the portal were the sentries we'd collected from the locations around Earth. My family followed, along with the Vaughns, the Lazaroffs, Sherus and his sister, and Mona—the rest of the GASP team had gone back to The Shade.

"I don't know. I don't suppose they've had a good night's rest since they arrived here."

"They'd want to know how it went," my mom said. "I think

in this instance we should wake them. Plenty of time to sleep when they're back where they *belong*."

My heart seemed to expand at her last words—the idea of having my children back home was unbelievably wonderful. To know that they were safe and sound in The Shade, far from the entity, ghouls, shadows and any other unpleasant creatures Nevertide had to offer.

"I also want to know if Benedict had any luck with the jinn. We'll need to find them before we leave," my father added, making his way toward the sleeping group before I could offer up another reason why we should leave them be. I wasn't sure I wanted to anyway—now this was all over, I was looking forward to getting back to normal family life as soon as possible. Well. Almost normal. I imagined there would be some sentries returning with us…

Caleb took my hand, both of us hurrying over to the children. I knelt beside Benedict, shaking him gently.

"What!" He sat up instantly, his eyes wild with fright.

"It's just us," I soothed, pushing back his hair. His body was trembling.

"Sorry," he murmured, "bad dream."

I nodded, feeling a pain in my chest. I hated that he'd seen so much, had been so afraid for so long that even his dreams were haunted. I could only hope that his fear would become a distant memory after he left this place.

Slowly all of them started to wake.

Ben and River flung themselves at Field, embracing him in a huge bear hug. I did the same with Hazel, and watched happily as Claudia wrapped both Ash and Ruby into an embrace. I didn't replicate my embrace with Tejus—I had the feeling he'd rather be left alone. However, it didn't stop me from feeling a strong parental affection for him.

We told them about the battle, how we'd finished off the shadow armies and the few ghouls that were left on Earth and done our best to restore a sense of normality to the cities—but in some cases, particularly Paris, the clean-up would take months. I hoped they'd eventually find a way to straighten the Eiffel Tower.

"What about the jinn?" Derek asked after the kids had had their fill of our stories.

Benedict looked about in agitation, as if he'd lost something, but then calmed down again as a very tall, willowy figure started to walk toward us. She'd been at the far end of the cove, and from the state of her hair and dress I thought that perhaps she'd been sleeping in the bushes.

She looked very lost. As she got closer, I recognized the strange dark runes shifting about like shadows on her arms… I'd seen something like them before.

An… Oracle?

Benedict started to tell us the story of how they'd found her in the Dauoa forests—a half-Ancient, half-jinni Oracle who had resided in Nevertide all her life. My instant reaction was one of skepticism—and even fear. I knew from *extreme* experience that Ancients were *not* something we should be messing around with. Had I known that she was here with my kids, I would have come back with them straight away…

Claudia glared at the woman, moving to stand in front of Ruby.

"She means no harm," Nuriya said wearily. "Admittedly her birthright is questionable, but I do believe she is a victim of circumstance—as far as I understand she has done nothing to harm any of us, and has no desire to do so."

"Queen Nuriya, with all due respect, I don't believe we can give an Ancient the benefit of the doubt," my father added, his jaw clenched tensely.

"Wait till you hear what she has to say," the jinni replied, "then judge her."

Queen Nuriya prompted the Oracle by taking her hand gently. The woman looked as if she was preparing to run off into the forest at any moment.

With a quiet, almost musical voice, the woman started to explain how she had come to Nevertide—how her parents had used the land to protect her, how they had cast the dome that Ibrahim and the other witches had found surrounding Nevertide and its ocean.

I did wonder what they had been protecting her *from*, but if she was the offspring of a jinni and an Ancient, then most likely it was their own species they felt she needed to be cut off from. To call Ancients conservative would be an understatement.

"What about the planet of the stones, the one in the In-Between?" my father asked after she had explained that she'd been responsible for locking the entity away.

The Oracle shook her head.

"That was my father's tribe. They knew the magic of the stones, which was passed on to me as a young girl. My father was responsible for the planet—he believed that it was the only way to render the ghouls powerless."

My father frowned. "It wasn't ghouls that escaped from those stones—it was the shadow."

"The shadow are ghouls," Benedict announced with a strange level of delight, "they're super ghouls—ghouls in their purest form! Tell them the history!" he demanded of the Oracle.

I suddenly felt queasy.

The Oracle frowned at my son.

"Benedict of The Shade, if you don't learn more courtly manners, you will find it a lot harder to get what you want in this life."

Benedict sighed. "Okay, *please* can you tell them about the history?"

"The creatures from the stones are the original ghouls, a lot stronger than the type you have come across before. When I arrived here, there were already supernatural creatures who had made Nevertide their home, and some of these were the regular, bone-like skeleton ghouls that you are so familiar with. I had been here a few years when the 'original' ghouls arrived. I do not know where they came from, perhaps somewhere far off in the In-Between. My father never found their home. The 'entity,' as you call him, the leader of the original ghouls, took over Nevertide. He built a fortress here in which to keep the memories of his victims. I had no bother from them, and they left me alone for the most part. That was until the human invaders came. They traveled by boat, and were fierce warriors. Even so, they were no match for the entity and his armies. Within a day the humans were made slaves. It was sad to see." The Oracle stopped for a moment, looking past us all, off into the distance as if she was watching her own tale unfold in front of her. With a dreamy sigh, she continued. "The future unfolded, and I didn't like what I saw. I helped the humans stage an uprising, I gave them weapons and asked them to consume the immortal water. They fought the entity, and I trapped him, knowing that many moons from that moment, there would perhaps be a time when he was set free."

"The sentries, where did they come from?" Benedict persisted. I nudged him, wondering why my son was being so impertinent, and so desperate to get to this part of the story.

"The sentries," the Oracle replied with a world-weary sigh, "are the result of humans who had become 'infected' by the original ghouls. The ghouls created their slaves to resemble their own powers and abilities, so they could create a species stronger than humans they could borrow mental power from. The sentries are hybrids, and share many skills of the original ghouls—things like long-sight, mind reading, and the ability to take 'mind matter' and turn it into something else—I believe you call these barriers?"

Tejus and Ash nodded silently.

"I didn't realize the ghouls had all of those abilities," my father cut in, his voice hoarse.

"The originals did. That is how they are able to take on the shape of the shadow—it is their own version of a barrier, a way to hide themselves. Of course, all these original ghouls took their power from their master in order to wake from the stones. Once he died, their powers left them, as I'm sure you saw."

"Hang on a second." Hazel held out her hand for us all to stop. "What you're actually saying is that—"

Oh God. Poor Hazel! I saw her slowly start to register what the Oracle was actually saying.

"Sentries are part ghoul!" Benedict cried gleefully.

"Hazel!" I exclaimed, before I could stop myself.

Oh, God.

My daughter glared at the Oracle.

"I-I don't believe you," she stammered.

"I'm sorry that you do not like it," the Oracle replied gently, "but it is the truth."

"Eeek!" Benedict made a silly, high-pitched noise that I assumed was meant to resemble a ghoul's cry and ran around the fire to escape the wrath of his sister.

"Benedict, I'm going to drown you in the ocean," she snapped furiously.

"Enough, Benedict!" my father and Caleb demanded simultaneously. He stopped instantly, and came back to stand beside me.

"You are in trouble when we get home," I snapped at him.

Tejus tried to comfort Hazel, but she seemed to be in a mild form of shock, just looking at the Oracle, then back at Tejus and Ash. She didn't say another word out loud, but just kept mouthing 'ghoul' as if trying to get used to the term. Oh, dear. I felt like we'd be having a *lot* of discussions about nature over nurture in the coming weeks. My heart went out to her. I had to admit, it was a difficult thing to accept—that my daughter had become part ghoul was a shock to us all. Of course, I would always love her, even if she started to hanker for digestive organs, but I doubted that it would come to that. If Tejus, Ash and the lovely girl Jenney were anything to go by, being a sentry was an accolade, not a curse.

"I want to ask about the stones again," my father interrupted.

"How did you and your father create them? The jinn of The Shade have lost this ability."

Queen Nuriya tilted her head in curiosity when the Oracle began to explain.

"The stones are created from the flowers the Hawk children delivered to you—they are a special breed that used to be popular with my kind for their energy. The flowers are used to crystallize them into a shell."

"And you are still able to accomplish this?" he questioned.

"I am," the Oracle agreed, "but please don't ask me what you are going to ask. I can see that you are hesitant to ask anyway— you still do not trust me. But I do not wish to return with you to The Shade. I cannot see my future if I do, and that frightens me."

"We need to learn from you," Queen Nuriya replied softly.

The Oracle lowered her head, and closed her eyes.

"Please," my father said. "There is a lot we could learn from one another. A lot of skills that the jinn have lost could be re-learned, and be of use to us in our line of work."

"I will need to think about it, but perhaps...perhaps it will be possible for a short while. I've never been anywhere but here. To visit a new dimension, and to speak with people—well, perhaps that would do me some good."

My father looked somewhat pleased, but mostly still wary. I knew that he and my mother, and the rest of the jinn, would be keeping a close eye on the Oracle if she did decide to return with us. We'd already had more than our fair share of Ancient trouble, enough to last ten lifetimes.

But perhaps, I reminded myself, looking at my daughter, who still appeared a little pale, *we shouldn't be so quick to judge the species, but rather to trust the individual.*

RUBY

I looked around my room, enjoying the moment of peace I had to myself before the celebrations started. The leaves rustled gently against the window panes, and the house felt still—no armies attacking us, no barriers up protecting me from the dangers that lay outside. My nights and days had been tranquil, and that had taken some getting used to.

We'd been back in The Shade for two weeks. When Derek and the other members of GASP had arrived the night that we'd slept on the sea shore, we hadn't even waited till dawn to leave. Ash and Tejus had both been willing to return with us, along with Zerus, Jenney and, after some reluctance, the Oracle. Ash had made sure the villagers were comfortable back at

Memenion's castle, but he'd been reassured by Queen Memenion that she would look after them, try to get them back on their feet before their emperor returned. Ash had trusted her, and so did I. After everything the sentries of Nevertide had been through, there was little ill-will left—it didn't matter who came from what kingdom, or where their allegiances had been before the battle. They were all ultimately going to be responsible for rebuilding their homeland.

I had worried about Ash adjusting to life in The Shade, but I needn't have. The initial fascination that he'd held with Earth when I first met him had returned quickly—he spent hours trying to understand television sets, blu-ray players and gaming consoles. Even ordinary household stuff like vacuum cleaners, blenders, the refrigerator—all held him under their spell. As a 'welcome to my world' gift, I'd taken him to Hawaii for the day, just to hang out. We went to the movies and saw the latest predictable blockbuster, but I doubted he even remembered what the film was about, he was so amazed by the sheer scale of the screen, the 'bizarre' outfits of the actors, and then there had been the snacks. I laughed to myself as I remembered having to physically drag him away from the self-service soda machine—the other movie-goers had already been staring at us because of Ash's size and his look of continued astonishment as he experienced what for everyone else was a typical Friday night.

After the movies, we'd gone to a restaurant—just a regular

diner—but Ash had sworn he'd never eaten so well in his life. While we walked along one of the piers, I noticed that Ash was practically buzzing with energy. I thought it was the mass amounts of sugar we'd consumed, but Ash sheepishly put me right—he'd been syphoning off pretty much everyone. It was like a free-for-all buffet being in public. I didn't really know how to react to that—it felt a bit unfair that innocent, unsuspecting humans were feeding him mentally, but then no one actually seemed to notice, or mind, so he couldn't have been feeding off any of them in large doses. I saved that as something to bring up again at a later date...

Tejus had also settled happily into life in The Shade. Where Ash fetishized the mundane human technology, Tejus was in awe of the weaponry and communications that GASP had at its disposal—things like the satellite maps, the radios, on-screen calls—anything that helped GASP in its missions. He had already become a useful asset—his more traditional war strategy skills were intriguing to both Benjamin and Derek. He would be a great future member of the GASP team.

I sighed. Looking at my bookshelves, I saw my childhood collection of combat manuals, Sun Tzu's *Art of War* and weapon guides. For so long I'd had my heart set on joining GASP. Now things were different. I had other obligations, a different life that was starting to take shape—one entirely unexpected, but that just made it all the more exciting.

In a few short hours, I would be getting married to Ash. We had our whole future together, one where I knew, thanks to the Oracle, that Ash wouldn't be coming to any harm—that our life together would be long and fulfilling. I couldn't wait to start it.

Earlier today I'd gone for a quiet walk in the forest. I still had the envelope that Varga had used for his letter to me, written moments before he'd been killed. I'd carried it around with me for a while—there was something comforting about the sight of his handwriting and his hurriedly-scrawled name on the back. I buried it under the earth, saying my final goodbyes. I loved Ash with all my heart, but Varga had meant something to me—and he would forever remain in my memory as a good man, one with integrity, whom I was glad to have known, even for such a brief time.

I glanced at myself in the mirror. Jenney, Yelena and Arwen had done an amazing job in transforming me from average human girl to extraordinary bride (even if I did say so myself). My make-up, courtesy of Arwen, who had become, in my opinion, the best make-up artist in The Shade, looked like it was hardly there—but it didn't stop my blue eyes from looking that much bluer, framed with dark brown mascara and just a hint of blusher on my cheekbones. My hair was worn down, falling in loose waves across my shoulders. Then there was my dress. I couldn't stop staring at it. The cut was simple—a plain sheath with delicate straps over each shoulder, with a small detailing of lace under my bust that showed off my figure while at the same time appearing suitably modest. The dress was more of an ivory-white, making my skin tone look warm. It was perfect—I was amazed at how '*un*-me' I looked, and how much—just for an evening—I was enjoying that.

Jenney was another one of the sentries who had settled in amazingly, in a way I wouldn't have anticipated. From the moment she arrived, she hadn't left Corrine's side. Magic and the power of the witches held endless fascination for her. She spent hours studying herbs and potions, remedies that belonged to ancient arts of healing—ones that didn't necessarily need innate witch powers to make them work. Admittedly, it hadn't always been a success. She'd managed to almost blow up the Sanctuary in an experiment gone wrong—something that Corrine hadn't been too pleased about, to say the least.

She had, however, been a huge help in getting the Murkbeech wards and the children who'd been kidnapped for the trials into a fit state to return home. It had taken a while—the kidnapped children were mostly suffering from post-traumatic stress, and needed care and attention more than any quick-fix spells. They would be leaving The Shade this evening, returning to their families, whom we had contacted already. Most were happy about it, perhaps with the exception of Yelena, who stubbornly claimed that she couldn't remember her address, or the names of her parents… I suspected that part of it was that she just couldn't bear to leave Benedict. Their friendship, which had grown as they had overcome the trials and dangers of Nevertide, was now stronger than ever—and I knew, as much as he vehemently denied it, that he would be heartbroken to see his friend go.

Tejus and Ash's friendship was also growing—the differences in class and status that had kept them apart in the past no longer had any bearing. As a result, they were learning to trust one another and let their personalities fall into sync—Tejus to laugh a bit more, Ash to not be so proud and testy. It was nice to see, and certainly made my and Hazel's lives easier.

Both of them had been living in the same residence, which helped the bonding process. Victoria, Bastien and Jovi went to stay with Vivienne and Xavier temporarily, freeing up a nearby treehouse for the two of them to use. I guessed Tejus had a hard time adjusting to the smaller living conditions—as spacious and beautiful as our treehouses were, they were small compared to the gray mass of Hellswan. But I knew Ash felt right at home.

I took one last look in the mirror, and tried to settle my racing heart. I was nervous, butterflies flitting around in my stomach, as I tried to comprehend the huge step I was taking toward the rest of my adult life. It was nerve-racking...and completely wonderful. I just wished Ash was with me now—he was the one who knew how to calm me down, who gave me perspective—who helped me be the person I wanted to be. The guy would soon be my *husband*.

"Hurry up!" Hazel's voice drifted in through my open window. "I'm nervous as it is—and you delaying us is *not* helping!"

I laughed. I couldn't remember ever hearing Hazel sounding so bossy...that was *my* job.

"I'm coming!" I yelled back, hurrying toward the terrace of my parents' treehouse. Hazel was leaning over the banister of her parents' nearby apartment, impatiently waiting for me to appear. She grinned when she saw me.

"You look *amazing*," she gasped.

"So do you!"

She did. Her dress, which Corrine had made—as she had mine—was a delicate white lace. It was a sheath cut like mine, but with long sleeves that finished at an elegant point over the back of her hands. The neck line was high, but the back low, and her dark hair, worn perfectly straight, trailed down her bare skin.

"Tejus is going to lose it," I added with a wink.

"Don't," she groaned. "I'm already worried that Dad's going to frown at me for how revealing the back is—he's the only one in my family who hasn't seen it yet."

I shook my head. The dress was beautiful, and I knew Caleb would just be dumbstruck at how mature and refined his daughter looked.

Grace and Rose stepped out from the doorway. Both of them waved at me and exclaimed over my dress and hair. I started to feel hugely self-conscious, belatedly realizing that this would be how it was all day—Hazel and I in the spotlight. I was glad we'd chosen to share our day with one another.

"Why are you still up there?" My mom appeared below us, on the forest ground, practically growling at the lot of us. "I have two very nervous grooms on my hands. They've started snapping at one another, and if you're even a second late I'm worried this wedding is going to descend into all-out war."

I glanced at Hazel, and we both burst out laughing—more out of nerves than anything else.

It was time to get a move on.

We all joined my mother on the ground. It would just be the four of us walking down the aisle —Hazel and I had decided against bridesmaids or maids of honor. The whole of The Shade would be in attendance, and that was enough for us. Hazel and I had always been close, but since Nevertide we had basically become inseparable. Aside from my family, she was the only other person who I truly *needed* to share this day with. I thought we both appreciated just how lucky we were to be at home, alive, and happy. It had been a long time coming.

We headed off toward The Shade's largest lake, where the ceremony would take place. Ash, Tejus, Zerus and Hazel had built a barrier over the water with their mental powers—so we'd literally be getting married *on* the water. Unexpectedly, it had been Tejus's idea. I guessed it was all part of him trying to get Hazel to embrace who she really was. After the initial shock of her being revealed as half-ghoul, she'd calmed down pretty quickly, especially as she honed her powers, realizing they were a gift rather than something she needed to be ashamed of. It was only Benedict who still delighted in teasing her about it—and in truth, I suspected he was just a bit jealous.

"I'm so proud of you," my mom murmured to me as we walked. She clasped my hand in hers, smiling up at me as she admired my dress for the millionth time. "Of you *and* Ash. I think that both of you have chosen so wisely. I just know that you're going to be happy—whatever you decide to do afterwards. Your happiness is all that's ever mattered to me and your father, you know that, right?"

"I know," I reassured her. "I love you, Mom."

She squeezed my hand. Her mention of 'whatever you do after' reminded me of the fact that Ash and I hadn't made any firm plans. Which, I guessed, was kind of typical of us both. We would be going on our honeymoon and then returning to The Shade for a short while for certain, but after that I just didn't know. Ash would need to get back to Nevertide—there was an entire land to be rebuilt, but I worried about spending time away from my family and friends.

"Are you all packed for tonight?" my mom asked suddenly.

"Yes!" I laughed. "I'm all packed—calm down. Everything's going to be okay, Corrine's going to be taking us after the ceremony."

"Not too early, though?" she replied.

"No—not too early. I promise."

Tonight.

My wedding night.

That was a whole *other* life-changing issue…

Hazel

The lake was breathtaking. After we'd created the barrier, the witches had insisted that we left the decorations to them. Now the lake had been transformed into a beautiful autumn-colored fantasy. Huge bouquets of dahlias, willow, viburnum berries and lilies were tied to every available surface. They were tied with ribbon and natural string to the backs of chairs. Trestle tables were situated on the shore of the lake where we'd be dining—and dancing—and more flowers and vines were woven around both the redwood trees and the wooden pagoda where the actual ceremony would take place. The air smelled heady and rich, the flowers mingling with the warm smell of bark and nature's own early fall scent.

The hushed and waiting crowd, the beauty of the lake and the smell in the air just reaffirmed for me that today was full of possibilities—the start of something new and exciting, an entire, unknown future waiting for me and Tejus to experience together. As much as I had been looking forward to today, it was the bit that came after which made my whole body tremble in anticipation—the nights and days of our honeymoon, and then all the time that would follow after, when we would start to build a life together.

Not long after we'd arrived home, Tejus had taken me aside one night and told me that he wanted us to live our lives here, at The Shade. He knew that Nevertide needed leadership, but that he wasn't the man best suited for the job. He was a warrior, and they needed someone to govern the land and help rebuild it. Someone who had the patience to deal with the politics, to be fair and kind, someone more empathetic than him. I thought that Tejus was doing himself a disservice, thinking he wouldn't be good at that role—I believed he would. But I also knew that he was better suited to helping GASP. Plus, I also thought Ben and my grandpa would have a *lot* to say about losing Tejus as one of their members. On hearing that we'd be spending the rest of our lives in The Shade, I had felt like my happiness was complete. I hadn't returned home that night. Tejus and I had spent the night under the stars, surrounded by fallen leaves and darkness, dreaming of our future together.

I looked around at the waiting crowd. Ahead of me, on the surface of the lake, Victoria bent down to say something to Bastien. As she did, I caught my first sight of Tejus standing at the altar.

My head spun.

We had spent so much time together in the weeks that we'd returned from Nevertide, but no matter how many days I spent in his company, each morning when I saw him for the first time, my stomach would twist inside me, my throat constricting as I became breathless with desire and a sense of wholeness—a feeling that had never abated from the moment I realized how I felt about him.

I watched his profile for a moment, noticing his sharp cheekbones and the harsh line of his jaw, the shadows of his deep-set eyes that always looked so intense—and irresistible. He turned to look at me, his eyes widening as he took in my appearance. His eyes became almost black with longing—I recognized the hooded gaze, it was one I knew so well. I felt heat rising up in my cheeks, my body feeling almost weightless.

"Breathe, Hazel." My father smiled as he came to stand next to me. He offered his arm, and I took it gratefully. I would need his strength to get down that aisle, to ground me when I thought I was going to float away. Everything just felt so *unreal*, and my happiness so total and complete that I thought it was just going to burst from my body in a brilliant light.

"Thanks, Dad," I whispered back.

"You look beautiful." His eyes were wet with unshed tears. He turned and glanced at my mom. A look passed between them that made my heart ache. I knew I was about to get married to the only being in all the dimensions with whom I could hope to experience a love as enduring and complete as my parents shared.

"We haven't spoken much about your time in Nevertide," he added in a hoarse voice, "and I know that some things are probably difficult to talk about—or don't need to be said. Your grandpa, mother and I have pieced a lot of it together through the children, Jenney and Zerus. It's not to interrogate you," he added hastily as I turned to him in surprise, "I just wanted you to know that I'm in awe of you. Both your mother and I are. You have grown into a magnificent woman, capable of protecting and caring for your friends and your brother, persevering when everything was against you. I know that you arranged for them to be sent home in your deal with Tejus— that you were willing to remain without them, to put their safety above yours. It takes compassion and bravery to do what you did, levels of which I'm not sure I possess. More than that, you also—amidst all the danger and uncertainty—learned to follow your heart. To love Tejus, to see the man behind your captor, to witness his flaws and love him anyway... I couldn't be prouder of you if I tried."

I nodded, unable to speak for a few moments as I tried to compose myself. His words meant so much. I'd always wanted to make my parents proud and to be a sister Benedict could look up to. To hear that I'd surpassed his expectations made me practically glow inside.

"You taught me to be this way." I gulped. "You and Mom. Whenever it *did* get hard, I always found that I could keep going, even when I didn't want to—and I know that came from the two of you. And I can only love because it's been given unconditionally to me."

I clasped his arm, wanting to remember this moment. Wanting to remember my dad's quiet strength next to me, the words that he'd said, and how I felt, waiting to walk toward my future.

"Are you ready?" he asked, glancing over at Yuri and Ruby.

We were ready.

The band started up, a sole flutist witch playing soft notes of a song I didn't recognize. Whatever it was, it was beautiful. The soft murmurings of the crowd faded to total silence, and they all turned to stare at Ruby and me as we crossed the water.

I was so happy to see so many faces of those I loved. I thought how lucky I was to be surrounded by friends and family—to have a life that was so full in a community of supernaturals and humans who were so unbelievably special. We'd all faced such adversity to get here, not just from our recent Nevertide adventure, but from all that we had struggled and fought through ever since my grandfather Derek founded our beloved island. We deserved all the moments of joy that we could grab— we all *deserved* days like this.

My gaze turned from the crowd to Tejus. He watched me approach, a soft smile on his face that looked slightly disbelieving, as if he was as amazed as I was that this was really happening.

We reached the pagoda, and my dad loosened his grip.

"Take care of her," he told Tejus, with a solemn expression.

"Always," Tejus replied, taking my hand gently.

He guided me up to the front of the altar, where Ibrahim was conducting the ceremony. The warlock smiled at all four of us, and gave a short speech welcoming everyone. I hardly heard a word he was saying. My body was so aware of Tejus's hand in mine, his broad frame brushing against mine.

I closed my eyes for a moment, feeling the breeze across my face.

I had been so anxious about this moment, so nervous. In that moment, the second that Tejus's hand had touched mine, I realized that I needn't have been. The ceremony was for my family and friends—it only served to make official what had already happened between us. Tejus and I had become one— heart, body and soul—when we had first made love. I was now as much a part of him as he was of me, and I could feel it, with every nerve in my body.

I reached out to him with my mind, wanting us in that moment to feel connected in every way possible. His energy was ready and waiting for mine, our bond strengthening as our minds entwined.

I'm in love with you, I said softly.

I'm in love with you too, he replied. *You're my life, Hazel. My heart wouldn't beat without you. I don't know what I did to deserve you, but I thank the gods for it, and I will spend the rest of my life loving you with everything that I have.*

I smiled up at him, and then turned back to Ibrahim.

"Do you have your vows, Hazel?" the warlock asked me.

"Yes, I do."

Sofia

I couldn't believe that I was watching my granddaughter and Ruby get married. It seemed like only yesterday that I was watching Caleb and Rose doing the same thing—and not *that* long since Derek and I were celebrating our own nuptials. I became overwhelmed by a sense that time was passing so quickly, years feeling like months, weeks passing in just a day. I supposed it was to be expected with the immortal lives we led; I was glad that it didn't make the precious moments seem fleeting. Some memories stayed with me forever, and life's ups and downs were just as important to me as a vampire as they had been as a human.

Rose squeezed my hand just at the moment that Hazel began

to speak her vows. In an unwavering, clear voice she addressed her husband.

"When we first met, you told me that you were selfish—so selfish that I couldn't possibly comprehend it. I'm telling you today that I *see* you, that what you deem selfish in yourself, I find the exact opposite. You are brave and loyal, generous and courageous, and your love for me is unlimited and unconditional—I know this, because I feel it. You have been my protector, my compass, my best friend and my mirror. In turn, I promise to love and cherish you—to hold and guard your heart, to be your guiding light, as you have been mine."

I brushed away a tear, the vision of Hazel in her white dress and her handsome sentry groom blurring. From her words, I sensed that she had found a love as deep and lasting as mine and Derek's. I was witnessing souls that were truly entwined, that would stand the test of time.

Tejus paused before returning his vows. I could see his jaw clenching slightly—the sign of a man unused to emotion and trying to repress it.

"Hazel," he replied in a hoarse voice, "being loved by you has been the most humbling experience of my life." He moved closer to her, gently pulling her toward him. The couple had become completely unaware of the rest of us, their audience invisible as they created their own bubble consisting of just the two of them. "I will spend the rest of my life trying to be worthy of you and your love. I offer myself to you completely. It was I who captured you, but it is you who has enslaved me. I am forever your lover, your servant, your friend—and I will remain so beyond my dying breath."

The couple kissed, Tejus's hand brushing against her jawline with the same reverence as if she were a precious jewel.

The ceremony continued, Ash and Ruby exchanging equally beautiful vows that tugged at my heart. All four of them had been through so much together, to see them come out the other side, stronger and more sure of themselves, was so life-affirming I could feel the entire audience being moved—the love displayed at the altar being shared by every single member of GASP in one way or another.

I looked around at the other guests. I could see Lucas and Marion with Avril, looking like a happy family unit—Avril's arms were wrapped around Lucas's neck as he held her up to see the ceremony. If that didn't show how transformative and altering love could be, then nothing did. It was lovely to finally see Lucas so content, and so dedicated to ensuring the happiness of his family. Jeramiah and Pippa, his wife, stood nearby, both families growing so much closer over time. Lawrence and Grace were standing behind me, both so happy to be home and finally able to get into the routine of their married life—the Nevertide mission had come so soon after their return from their honeymoon, there had hardly been time to adapt to their newly married status at The Shade.

I heard a sharp whisper, and looked over to see Brett and Bella with their adopted ogre kids who had been rescued from the harpies. Bella was trying her best to keep the little scamps under control. I laughed softly to myself. Derek and I were fortunate that Ben and Rose had been fairly easy as children. It was only when they'd grown up that they became a handful. All the fear, the worry, and the anxiety as they both navigated the supernatural world...let's just say if I wasn't an immortal I'd have quite a few gray hairs on my head. It had all been worth it, of course—watching them grow into adults with children of their own gave me and their father pleasure that we'd never even anticipated. The love and strength of our family just seemed to grow.

Jeriad's son Heath had also come for the day, traveling from the Hearthlands. It was good to see him again, and I wondered if we'd be seeing more of him in the future after he neared the end of his celibacy vow. He was such a good kid, and his rugged good looks were developing more with age, something that the younger female residents of The Shade hadn't failed to notice.

Arwen and Brock were holding hands, standing so close you couldn't fit a dime between them. I also spied Orlando, standing near Regan—his eyes flitted over to her continuously throughout the ceremony, while Azaiah glanced at him occasionally, looking unsettled. Near the dragons stood Aisha,

Horatio and Riza, the little girl held between her parents; they were obviously elated to be reunited with her, both of them looking down lovingly as she merrily chatted away to herself, sweetly oblivious to what was going on around her. My dad and Kailyn were standing with Hunter, another rescue from the harpy orphanage. The werewolf cub was doing well, his new parents blossoming along with him. It warmed me in ways I couldn't express to see how Hunter brought out the tender side of my father.

The music started up again, and the two couples made their way back along the aisle. Corrine and Mona had created special 'confetti' for all of us—each guest had been given a small paper box to be opened at the end of the ceremony. I lifted the flap of mine, and laughed in delight as four butterflies danced up into the air. They were joined by hundreds of others, their bright wings creating a beautiful, kaleidoscopic drape over the newly-weds.

We all followed them out to the lake's shore. Amidst the cheering and wolf-whistles, Hazel and Ruby threw their bouquets up in perfect unison. Rose and I jumped back, along with some of the other mothers, while the younger GASP members rushed forward in a delighted frenzy. There were screams of laughter as Field caught Hazel's—well, it was more of a case of the falling flowers landing in his arms. He rolled his eyes, trying to push it on to one of the more enthusiastic girls, but they wouldn't let him. Maura, standing next to him, blushed furiously—even more so when Orlando gave her a sly wink.

I noticed Queen Nuriya and Sherus standing near one of the trestle tables, and started making my way over. Sherus had remained on the fire planet after returning briefly to Nevertide, and I hadn't expected him to return to The Shade. It had come as a surprise to us all when not only had he returned, he had stayed on these last two weeks, spending most of his time with the jinni queen. Their unlikely friendship had surprised us all; clearly there was a romance blossoming there, and I was glad— Nuriya deserved to find love and her own happy ending after all the trauma she'd been through, losing her love along with every other male member of her family, and all she had done for us.

Standing near them, but slightly out of the way, was the Oracle. She had remained in The Shade far longer than we had expected her to. She would be off after the ceremony today, but hadn't told us whether she'd be returning to Nevertide or not. She looked imposingly beautiful, wearing a dress that Corrine had lent her, one that set off her impossibly pale skin and white-blonde hair. The strange dark markings danced across her skin. She had explained to us that they represented time—the ever-changing moments of the past and the future, forever etched onto her memory. She seemed slightly sad today, and I wondered if it was because she'd be leaving us.

It had taken a while for many of The Shade's residents to

warm up to her—the usually kind-hearted River in particular. She remembered the Oracle sisters too well, but no one could forget the Ancients. Still, most had come to accept the Oracle— she was too kind and gentle for many to be put off for long. I couldn't help but feel a great deal of compassion for her. Living up in that mountain for most of her life, in complete solitude, was a horrific concept, one I wouldn't wish on my worst enemy.

I called out a 'hello' to the Oracle, and she smiled back at me. I knew she wouldn't come over and talk, but that was fine. She still liked to keep mostly to herself.

Moving my way through the crowd, I bumped into Zerus, Tejus's brother.

"H-hello," he mumbled. "You look beautiful today, Sofia."

I smiled up at him, always charmed by his sweet nature. I'd grown increasingly fond of him since he'd arrived at Nevertide, and though (to my amusement) his attentions toward me irritated Derek to no end, I understood them for what they were; Zerus was an orphan who, despite his age, still searched for a mother-type figure.

"Thank you, Zerus. Did you enjoy the ceremony?" I asked.

"I'm very happy for Tejus and your granddaughter." He nodded. "They make a beautiful couple. I'm glad my brother has found peace at last."

I nodded, hoping that Zerus wouldn't be far behind. Perhaps if he remained with us at The Shade he would find whatever it was he was looking for. I wasn't sure what his plans were though—he refused to sleep in any of the accommodations we provided, insisting that he would prefer to stay out with the stars. I imagined that Zerus was a nomad at heart—perhaps he wouldn't stay for long—but I wanted him to know he always had a home here should he need it.

"I hope you find peace too, Zerus," I said gently.

"As do I." He smiled softly and then was gone, swallowed up by the crowd.

Suddenly my husband reappeared, smiling down at me with a knowing look in his eyes.

"I take it you'll be wanting to dance?" he asked, offering me his hand.

"Of course," I said with a wry grin.

My stomach flipped over as his piercing blue eyes raked over my attire. Another thing that I wished for my granddaughter that I'd wished for my own daughter too—though would never have said so—was a husband who, even after thirty or so years, still sent molten desire running through their veins. Just like mine did.

"What are you thinking?" Derek asked me, arching a daring brow as I fell silent.

"Nothing," I replied sweetly. "Absolutely nothing… Shall we dance?"

TEJUS

Lights hung in the sky, seemingly suspended in thin air. They cast a hazy glow over the guests in the inky blue twilight, and lit up the dewy skin of my wife's cheekbones and made her brown eyes golden.

"You put the stars to shame, Hazel," I breathed in her ear. She looked indescribably beautiful, and all day I had been unable to tear my eyes away from her, still unable to comprehend that she was mine. My *wife*. That I would get to wake up next to her every day for the rest of my life.

"You are more romantic than I ever gave you credit for," she replied, a small smile playing on her lips. She moved her hand to my shoulder, drawing her body closer. We were dancing—

the first dance, shared with Ruby and Ash.

"Don't get closer," I murmured.

Her cheeks flushed, and the smile turned into a self-conscious laugh.

"Sorry," she whispered.

"You will be. Later."

"I'm taking my romantic comment back," she replied archly.

"It's not romantic to want to make love to my wife?"

She paused, smiling quickly at Vivienne, who was standing nearby as we turned.

"When you put it like that…" she whispered.

I laughed, moving her closer to me anyway because I couldn't bear not to. The music picked up, and other couples began to join us on the dance floor. I'd never been around so many happy, relaxed people—not just today, but during the two weeks that we'd been residing in The Shade. It had taken some getting used to. Ash teased me about sleeping with a dagger under the mattress, but some habits were hard to break. But it was starting to feel like I could be truly content—not just when I was around Hazel, but in all manner of ways. It was a life that I had never envisioned, a future that I hadn't mapped out. I thought about my mother; perhaps she had been able to foresee how different my life could be without the chains of Hellswan around my neck, how love might alter me. I knew Varga had hoped for this – for me, and possibly for himself too. What neither of them could have predicted was me finding the missing piece of my soul in another—or just how profound that love could be.

"You've gone somewhere. Come back to me." Hazel jolted me back to the present with a teasing smile.

"I was thinking about my mother, and Varga. They would have liked this. I think it's what they wanted for me all along."

Hazel nodded. "I don't know about your mother, but yes, I think it's what Varga would have wanted for you. Zerus is happy for you too, you know."

I grimaced. Hazel had done her best to build the bond between my brother and me, but it was difficult. We were both so unused to one another, strangers almost, in a way. Our father had spent so long preparing all his sons for our ultimate competition, that we no longer seemed to have any common ground, or a way to make that different. But perhaps time would change that—and a very persuasive wife.

"I know he is." I sighed. "I hope he stays here for a while. It would give us a chance, at least."

"You should tell him."

"Perhaps I will," I replied, silencing her with a kiss. Those soft lips melted into mine, her body becoming pliant and willing. I let out a throaty chuckle—I was pushing my luck. Caleb and I were slowly making inroads with one another, but mauling his daughter on the dance-floor at our wedding might have been pushing the vampire too far.

To distract my willing wife, I spun her around and found us dancing next to Julian and Jenney—their inexperienced steps and Julian's slightly-too-large suit rendered them endearing. I was glad that Jenney had returned to The Shade with Ash, and would be returning to Nevertide with new skills, perhaps replacing Abelle's version of healing with a more honest practice.

"Excuse me," a soft voice came from behind me. I stopped dancing, and, to my surprise, turned to see the Oracle. She was looking at us both expectantly – in her strange way of looking at something, and past something at the same time.

"I haven't given you your gift yet," she continued before either of us could say a word. "It is a mixed gift, but a gift nevertheless."

"Honestly, you don't need—"

The Oracle cut Hazel off. "But you see, I do. It is imperative that I do." She placed both her hands over Hazel's flat stomach—it was a brief touch, lasting no more than a split second, but it enraged me.

"What are you *doing*?" I snapped at her.

"As I said. A wedding gift. Your tribe is strong and powerful. As your child will be."

Before we could react, she turned away, her white hair glowing brilliantly under the lights for a few moments before she vanished into the crowd.

"Don't worry," Hazel said, though she looked quite unnerved

herself as she touched her stomach. "I-I'm sure it's nothing. I think she means well."

"I *am* worried."

"I think she's just a bit odd. That was probably her way of congratulating us… maybe blessing our future children?" Hazel wet her lips and then shrugged, apparently dismissing the matter.

Hm. Perhaps I was overreacting. There were lots of things I didn't understand about the supernatural world—especially when it came to witches and jinn. Even in the short time I'd been in The Shade, their abilities had frequently astounded me and I was starting to realize how little I knew about the dimensions and the creatures they were home to.

"All right," I muttered, glancing around to see if the Oracle would reappear. I saw nothing, and turned my full attention back to my wife.

"Tejus." She leaned up, whispering in my ear. "When do you think it's okay for us to leave?"

I laughed. "You're the bride, it's anytime you wish."

"Soon, please."

"Now soon?" I asked.

"Now soon," she confirmed with a grin.

"Let's say our goodbyes."

We hastily made our way around the guests, thanking them for coming, and accepting their heartfelt congratulations. I stood back as Hazel embraced one of her friends, and caught sight of the Oracle again…

This time, she was standing next to both Grace Conway and Victoria Blackhall, placing her hands intermittently on both their stomachs. I was about to march over and demand to know what she was doing, but before I could move she had fled once again. Grace and Victoria gave one another puzzled glances and then shrugged, like Hazel had done. Clearly they didn't think it was a big deal either.

I was about to re-join my wife, when Rose appeared at my side.

"Tejus," she said, her green eyes warm and welcoming. "I'm thrilled that you're joining our family. You've made my daughter so happy, and her father and me."

"Thank you," I replied, clearing my throat awkwardly. Without warning, she rose upward on her tiptoes, and embraced me tightly. I felt a lump forming in my throat. There was something about her – perhaps the hair, her perfume or her slender frame, that reminded me of my own mother.

"I'm glad to be joining your family too," I muttered, breaking away from the embrace. She smiled broadly up at me.

"Good," she replied. 'You'll do us all proud."

"Are you ready?" Hazel asked, appearing next to her mother. I smiled in relief. I had experienced enough emotions for one day.

I glanced back once to where the Oracle disappeared, and then fixed my focus once again on my beautiful wife. *Now isn't the time for wondering about that strange creature.*

"I'm ready," I said.

The Oracle was forgotten as we made our way toward Shayla. She would be transporting us to our honeymoon destination— a secret that had been kept from me. Not that I minded in the slightest; as long as Hazel was by my side, I would have gone anywhere.

RUBY

I gazed out at the snow-capped mountain in the distance. The sun was starting to set, the sky blazing in a beautiful red hue. We were in the highlands of a remote Tibetan valley. I had known that Ash would have his work cut out for him when we returned to Nevertide, and I had wanted our honeymoon to be as peaceful and relaxing as possible.

We were staying in a renovated farmhouse that still maintained elements of old-world tradition—like the handcrafted wooden bathtub, and the rich hues of red and copper that made up the charming décor.

Our farmhouse was adjacent to an old temple that now served as a luxury spa. Corrine and I had made sure that we would be the only guests staying that week—we had the facilities to ourselves, and no one around for miles to disturb us. It was heaven.

"Ash?" I called, stepping out onto the terrace.

He turned to face me, relaxing in a wicker chair that looked out over the valley. A pot of mint tea was brewing next to him, and the smell wafted through the air on the fresh breeze.

"It's incredible here, Shortie." He smiled, opening his arms for me to join him. I came and sat on his lap, leaning against his chest as I took in the magnificent views.

"It really is." I sighed with contentment.

We sat in silence for a while. We had arrived in the early afternoon, due to the time difference, and now I felt drowsy—completely overwhelmed by the events of the last twelve hours. My mind drifted back to our wedding ceremony. Ash's eyes had fixed on mine as he had gently taken my hand, the breeze swaying the tendrils of his hair. My family, friends, the sparkling water, the beautiful redwoods and Ibrahim had ceased to exist. He had spoken his vows in a low voice – unwavering and more sure than I'd ever heard him. *"You saved me from death and darkness. From losing myself and everything that I am. You have always brought me back into the light – have given me reason to keep going when it seems like everything is lost. I love you, Ruby. And I will always love you, till the end of time."*

Ash and I had an eternity to be together, and it was at the

ceremony when that had first hit home properly. A bubble had swelled inside my chest, one of disbelieving happiness that still hadn't dissipated…and I wondered if it ever would.

"We're husband and wife," I murmured eventually, coming back to the present and stating the fact with astonishment. I felt like I was dreaming; the scenery, the quiet time with Ash with no danger lurking in the distance…it all felt so unreal.

"We are," he breathed, running his lips softly down my neck. His arms closed around me, and I felt my insides melt.

Before we could go any further, and I was carried away in a haze, I refocused.

"Ash, there are some things I need to tell you," I began, speaking slowly so I could find the right words.

"That doesn't sound good."

The kissing of my neck paused, and I turned toward him in alarm.

"No! It *is* good news, I'm just trying to get this out properly—and I guess I'm not. I wanted to talk about Nevertide, about us going back."

He was silent for a few moments, and then he sighed against me.

"I don't want to talk about that. Not now. I just want to be with you. Let's enjoy the time we have."

I half-laughed. I was making such a mess of this.

"That's what I mean. I want us to start our life in Nevertide.

It doesn't mean never returning to The Shade. I'd like to come and go when we want to, but to have Nevertide as our home."

"Do you mean that?" he replied in a broken tone.

"Of course."

I looked him deep in the eyes. I wanted him to know how serious I was about this—that living in Nevertide was no hardship if he was there.

"What about GASP... your life in The Shade?" he questioned.

"We'll still be members of GASP. We'll just live in Nevertide, like many dragons live in The Hearthlands. And my life in The Shade would be nothing without you, Ash. You're my husband. How could I not live by your side? Leaving you to rebuild Nevertide on your own? I want that to be something we do together."

Ash drew his thumb down the side of my face, his eyes searching mine in wonderment.

"You're incredible, you know that?"

"You keep telling me," I whispered in reply.

He kissed me, long and lingering, his hands snaking up into my hair and then pulling my backside closer toward him. My body felt like it was on fire—I wanted him *so* much. Not just in my mind, but in the pure, physical sense.

"Wait." I pulled back. "There's more. And we should talk about it, before..."

"I know what this is about." He smiled gently at me. "And we don't have to do a thing. I *like* our unique way of being intimate. Nothing else matters."

I shook my head. It mattered to me.

"I want to do this properly, Ash. I want us to make love as husband and wife. I spoke to Corrine and Mona about…this at length." I blushed. That had been a seriously awkward conversation that I *never* wanted to repeat. "And they say I should still be able to turn into a vampire even if I become a sentry—become a hybrid. And the offer is always open to you too, whenever you want it."

"You're willing to become a sentry?" he asked hoarsely. "Part *ghoul?* To deal with the hunger and everything that Hazel went through?"

"It's not that different to turning into a vampire, and I know you'll help me through it. I've got friends and family around me who will support my decision as well, so it's going to be a different experience to the one that Hazel had."

His caresses became firmer, his hands moving up my waist and then running across my stomach and hips.

"Are you sure about this?" he asked again, his voice growing huskier.

"I'm one hundred percent sure…" Draping my arms around his neck, I pressed my cheek against his and whispered in his ear, "Take me to bed?"

He gulped, lifting me up as he stood out of the chair. He put me in a fireman's carry, and I laughed, banging on his back for him to put me down. Ignoring me, he walked through to the bedroom. There, he laid me down on the low bed. The sheets were a cool silk, the perfect counterpart to my flaming skin.

He untied my dressing gown, kissing my bare skin.

"My wife," he breathed, branding me with his lips before shedding his clothes and lowering himself on top of me.

I felt the moment, clearly, when I was about to transform. My breath hitched, a strangled cry of bliss burning my throat.

I love you.

The thought rang as clear as a bell, and I felt my soul lifting from my body. I was weightless, and in that moment of neither belonging to my body or my mind, my husband's soul entwined with mine. I sank back into myself, feeling like I was falling deeper and deeper into the warmth of the earth. When I opened my eyes, I saw Ash gazing back—his gorgeous brown eyes hooded with desire, his hair mussed and lips flushed, sweat beading on his taut muscles—and I knew that from that moment on, he would forever be a part of me.

HAZEL

We lay entangled in the sheets of our four-poster bed. Outside, despite it only just being the end of summer, winds whipped at the window panes, the craggy Scottish landscape making our room seem all the more comforting and cozy. A roaring fire was dancing away in the hearth, sending flickers of light across the stone walls and the elaborate tapestries that hung from the walls.

Tejus's fingers idly ran up and down the curve of my bare waist, sending shivers running through to my toes. We had arrived hours ago, and not left from the bed since Tejus had whisked me to it. I had high hopes that we wouldn't need to for many more hours to come.

"When did we leave Nevertide?" he asked lazily, a note of

laughter in his voice.

"Two weeks ago," I replied.

"And you're already missing castles and stone walls?"

"I wanted to give you a taste of home," I whispered, leaning in to kiss his neck. "I know you're not planning to go back... I thought you might miss it."

"I love it here," he replied, dragging my body closer to his, "but the best thing about Nevertide was you. Don't worry about me missing it. You're my home."

I buried my head in his chest, embarrassed to show him how deeply his words affected me. I felt like my heart was going to burst into a million pieces. I recalled the first time I realized I had feelings for Tejus—how a moment like this would have been completely unbelievable to me then. How the future we were just about to embark on, and the promises we'd just made to one another, would have seemed impossible.

I had thought that I would overcome my feelings for him somehow. They had been so fragile and dangerous that I'd tried my best to ignore them. In his arms now, I could look back at them with a different perspective, relishing each moment where he had sparked something inside me, made my heart beat that little bit faster, or wounded me so deeply that I felt I couldn't breathe. All the pain, the joy, the awkward in-betweens, it had been worth it. They had created what we were now.

Memories like his fierce hug at the arena after he had

destroyed the disk came flooding back to me, his disapproving look when he caught me talking to Nikolay before the honesty trials, the first time I had seen him naked in the labyrinth—and how my body had flooded with white-hot heat. The feeling of his body brushing against mine as he found me in the forest, blindfolded and bound. Our first kiss. Our first night together.

"You're my home too," I murmured against his skin.

"Are you thinking about when we first met?" he asked curiously.

I laughed. "Yes, can you tell?"

"It's coming through your energy…I can see images in my mind that don't belong to me," he replied.

"We're mind-melding?" I questioned. I hadn't been aware that we were doing it.

"No, I don't think so." He frowned. "I think as we get closer, it's easier to pick up your emotions and thoughts…interesting."

"*Helpful*," I corrected. "You'll know when you're in trouble."

"I doubt I need mind-melding skills for that," he replied dryly.

The mention of the sentry abilities reminded me of a question that I'd wanted to ask him.

"Does it bother *you* that you're a ghoul hybrid?" I asked. The subject had never really come up, and I'd just assumed that he was fine with it—that it was unavoidable, and therefore tolerated.

"Not really." He sighed. "I think it explains why they were always able to wound us so badly—when they clawed or bit us, they must have passed across something that reacted to our own genetic make-up. That ghoul wound I received at the ridge took so long to heal."

"I remember," I replied, tracing the scar on his chest. It joined with the one Ash had given him on his pectoral—the symbol of the commander of the six armies. To me, they were both evidence of his bravery and sacrifice.

"I keep thinking how things might have turned out differently if the Oracle had come down from her mountaintop," I continued. "You would have known about the ghouls, known about the entity. More would have lived."

"Perhaps," he agreed. "But there's no point in looking to the past. What's done is done. I don't have many complaints about the way it's turned out…"

"I know," I agreed, "you're right. Forward looking only."

I grinned up at him, but his eyebrows were raised in an expectant look.

"So what will it be?"

"The future?" I frowned, sitting up.

"Our future."

I chewed on my lip, considering his question. There were so many things I wanted Tejus and I to experience, I hardly knew where to start.

"Well," I began hesitantly, looking over at the fire. Beyond living in The Shade and becoming fully-fledged members of GASP, we hadn't really discussed what we might want from our personal lives.

"Children. That would be good, at some point," I replied softly. He was silent, and I risked glancing up at his face. There was so much tenderness there that, for a moment, my heart felt like it had stopped.

"Of course," he replied. "At least seven."

What?

"I'm joking, two is fine."

"Not funny," I gasped.

"It was if you saw your expression. But yes, I want children with you. Of course I do. You'll make an amazing mother... I just hope they turn out like you."

"And not you?" I replied. "My opinion is *very* different."

"What else?" he asked wryly, swiftly changing the subject.

"Regular vacations like this?" I laughed. "Days spent curled up in bed...no food, no water..."

He growled. "You need to eat."

I nodded. I was starting to feel light-headed; rather than draining the energy of my husband, it would be a good idea to get some sustenance in me.

"I'll find us some," he replied quickly, moving to get up.

"You can just call them—on the telephone thing I told you

about," I replied, sinking back into the pillow that he'd just vacated.

"I'm growing to like this world," he mused, moving across the room.

I lay back, thinking about the kind of children that Tejus and I might have. My hand briefly fluttered over my stomach, and my mind was drawn back to the Oracle's actions earlier…what *had* she been doing?

BEΠEδICⱦ

Ash, Ruby and Jenney were getting ready to leave The Shade. The couple had returned from their honeymoon a few days ago, and spent most of their remaining time with Ruby's family. I was sad to see them go. I couldn't understand how Ruby was willing to return to Nevertide... and that decision had pretty much put me off love forever. She had clearly gone insane. Who in their right mind would return to the ripped skies, the earthquake-destroyed kingdoms and the home of the Impartial Ministers? Not only that, but she'd also voluntarily become a sentry—a half-ghoul! Yeah. Ruby was a head case, and all because she'd fallen in love.

She kept telling us all—mainly me, Hazel and Julian, who

were the ones who questioned her decision the most—that she would return regularly and that she and Ash would put Nevertide back together, piece by piece.

I knew that my grandpa and Ben were pleased about the decision. Having sentry allies was going to be a big help to GASP—some of their skills, like True Sight and the barrier-building, were particularly helpful.

"Have you got everything?" Claudia asked Ruby for the millionth time.

"I've got everything, Mom." She smiled wearily. "Don't worry—honestly, we'll be back before you even have time to miss us."

"I miss you already, sweetheart," Claudia moaned.

Pretty much the whole of GASP were gathered to watch them go. We stood, waiting to get our own goodbyes in while Claudia fussed around her daughter.

"She's going to be all right," Yuri said, gently squeezing his wife's shoulder. "We can go and visit them too, you know."

"I know," Claudia sighed, her eyes red-rimmed.

"Hey, you." Ruby gave me a fierce hug while her mom and dad were distracted. "I'm going to miss you a whole lot. I've gotten used to having you around—Nevertide won't be the same without you."

I laughed loudly. "Yeah, sure, what's Nevertide without a possessed kid, right?"

"Exactly." She grinned.

Ash came up behind her, holding out his hand to me. "You're welcome anytime. It's your home too."

I shook his hand, privately thinking that I *never* wanted Nevertide to be described as my 'home'.

"Thanks, Ash," I replied instead with a smile.

They said their goodbyes to Julian, who looked slightly red-cheeked as Ruby gave him another fierce hug. She knocked his glasses askew, so when the two finally broke apart, Julian looked rumpled and flustered.

"What's with you?" I asked.

"Nothing," he hissed.

Jenney said her goodbyes next, and I realized that I'd probably miss her as much as I would Ruby. I hoped she would return to The Shade one day—her almost blowing up the Sanctuary had been *cool*. When she went to hug Julian goodbye, he blushed an even darker shade of red than before. I rolled my eyes.

"Wish you were all coming as a clean-up crew," Ash remarked to some of the witches behind me. I smiled to myself. I bet he did—they were going to have a massive job on their hands.

"Actually, that's not a bad idea…I've got a couple of creatures in need of a bit of community service." My grandma Sofia smiled to herself. "I'll be back in a moment, don't leave."

She dashed off in the direction of the Black Heights. I

shrugged, turning back to Jenney.

"Have you seen Yelena?" she asked. "I said goodbye to her earlier, but I thought she'd be here for the send-off."

"I haven't, sorry." But I guessed where she'd be. Mom had finally tracked down her address, and she was meant to be leaving this afternoon. Yelena would no doubt be hiding somewhere, trying to postpone the inevitable, like she'd been doing since the moment she got here. I didn't know why she was missing this send-off though, she'd only be annoyed later when she discovered they'd gone.

"What's your grandma got?" Ash murmured, looking back in the direction of The Shade.

I grinned, instantly recognizing the host of brownies who had been jailed in the caves. Julian and I had found out about them a week ago, and heard the whole 'Minotaur' mystery story from Corrine.

"I think you just found your clean-up team." I laughed. The brownies looked *seriously* displeased.

"Brownies," announced my grandma. "You'll need to keep a close eye on them, but I'm hoping that after some honest labor they'll improve. If not, feel free to send them back." She glared down at the ring-leader, who sniffed angrily and kicked a pebble with her foot.

"I hope there's better food there than there is here," the brownie grumbled.

I laughed out loud at that.

Dream on!

Shayla and a group of other witches were also sent along to help with the clean-up. I hoped for Ruby's sake that with the witches' magic, things would be resolved quickly. I hoped that she and Ash did create the changes in Nevertide that they were hoping for. Ash had major plans to abolish the kingdoms, and have one central, truly democratic government—it would mean he would abdicate his throne, but he was insistent that it would be worth it. I wasn't sure I'd want to give up being emperor of an entire land, even if it was just Nevertide.

Eventually, with witches and brownies in tow, the three sentries left The Shade.

"This sucks." Julian sighed.

"I know," I agreed.

I needed to go and look for Yelena. My mom would start panicking soon, and then Yelena might never be allowed to visit again—and that would make Yelena so upset, it wasn't worth the drama and tears.

"I need to hunt down Yelena," I told Julian.

"Want help?"

"No, I'm okay," I replied quickly. She was so stubborn, if she had an audience it would only make her act out more.

* * *

It took me absolutely ages to find her. My legs and arms had been shredded by the undergrowth in the forests, but my initial hunch had been right. Sitting on a branch of a low-hanging tree on the outskirts of the treehouse residences was Yelena.

"You are a *pain!*" I yelled up at her.

"I don't care. I'm not leaving." She crossed her arms, her face set in a furious expression.

"You know you can't stay here, right? That you do actually have parents who are probably out of their minds with worry?"

"No, they're not."

I sighed. She was *impossible.* We'd already had this argument a million times—even the Hawk boys had gotten involved, *again,* after our last night in Nevertide. You'd think, as they'd been orphans, they would have been able to talk some sense into her, but apparently not.

"You can come back and visit, I already told you that," I called up, pulling out my trump card.

"I don't want to visit. I want to live here. I like it here! I like the witches, the Hawks, the vampires, the werewolves, everyone. Zerus gets to stay, and the Oracle hasn't gone anywhere, why do I have to be the one who leaves?"

"All the other kids have gone!" I exploded. "Why can't you be excited like they were? They couldn't wait to go home— you're the only one who's being weird about it!"

"Just let me stay!"

I leaned against the tree. I was hungry and thirsty and irritated. I'd never met anyone so difficult. I didn't understand what her deal was. The whole time we were in Nevertide she'd been up for anything—I mean, she'd always been *annoying*, but she'd been generally happy to follow the ill-fated 'Hell Rakers' *and* me while I was possessed…but suddenly returning home was completely beyond her?

Realizing I was getting nowhere, I started to climb the tree. After more scrapes, and a bruise on my shin that hurt like hell, I arrived on her branch and came to sit down next to her. She didn't look in my direction.

From here, I could see that her face was tear-streaked and her eyes were as red as Claudia's had been.

"What's really the matter?" I muttered.

She took a deep breath, then swung her legs in agitation. "Like I said—"

"No. What's going on?" I asked again. "Just tell me the truth. I can't read your mind, you know."

"I… I'm worried that I'll forget," she replied in a small voice. "That I'll just think this was all make-believe—none of it really happened, and that The Shade doesn't exist. I'll go to boarding school, and I'll grow up. I'll become boring like my parents, and only care about paying the mortgage and how much fuel's in the tank. I'll forget you, and Julian and the others. I'll forget how *awesome* it was."

"You don't need to forget." I rummaged around in my pocket. "Here, take these. They're my treasures. I took them from Nevertide…like mementos. But you can have them, if you like."

I held out my hand, showing her the Viking coin I'd taken from one of the chests by the cove, and the broken ghoul stone. I also had a chip of emerald crystal I'd found when we went back to visit Hellswan after it was destroyed.

She smiled.

"Really?" she asked softly.

"Yeah. Keep them. They can remind you when you forget."

I swallowed, suddenly feeling very uncomfortable with the way Yelena was looking at me, with her massive blue eyes and rosy pink cheeks.

I cleared my throat. "I'll come looking for you when I'm a vampire anyways," I said gruffly, "so you'd better watch out… Don't go down any dark alleyways."

She beamed.

"Thanks, Benedict," she said, her eyes twinkling.

I shrugged. I didn't know why she had to make such a big *deal* out of it.

"No worries."

DEREK

I wandered atop the Black Heights, enjoying a rare hour of solitude and the early-autumn breeze—barely discernible down below, but up here on the mountains it whipped at my hair and shirt.

Gazing down over our magnificent island, I smiled to myself. Our family was growing. My eyes drank in the scene below: the still beaches where the ocean gently lapped at the shore, the lighthouse on the coast—Sofia's and my sacred space, its proud structure still weathering every storm—the Vale, safe and humming with its human residents, the meadows and fields that provided us with ample agricultural land, and the redwoods that scattered the island, their mighty branches gently swaying in the wind.

We had worked hard to make The Shade what it was today: a safe haven for all, regardless of species.

A movement caught my eye, disrupting my reverie. I turned toward a low rockery, part concealed on the north-facing mountain range.

"Who goes there?" I questioned.

I received no reply, but a few moments later, a figure with a cascade of white-blond hair stepped into view. It was the Oracle. She clambered up to where I stood, and I waited patiently for her to explain what she was doing up here – while admiring her ability to maneuver herself across the rocks when she lacked 'normal' vision.

"Forgive me for the intrusion." She sighed. "I've been coming up here to think. It's become a habit, I suppose."

I nodded. Having spent her entire life on the mountain range by the Dauoa forest, it didn't surprise me that this was where she would feel most at home.

"You're not bothering anyone," I replied simply. I had grown to respect the Oracle, despite her awkward ways—we had one thing in common at least: a desire to walk and brood.

"I'm glad I found you here," she continued, her voice lilting and soft. "There are some things I wish to discuss with you... things I'm not quite sure I understand myself."

I nodded. "About your past?"

The Oracle had been vague on the matter of her childhood, and what her life had been like before she'd been sent to Nevertide. There were things she could remember of the jinni clan that her father hailed from, like the making of the stones, but other parts remained hazy. At first I had assumed it was her own desire to remain secretive, but as time had gone on, I started to believe that she'd had certain parts of her memory wiped, perhaps by her parents. Still, that was a far-fetched hypothesis. To wipe part of the memory of an Oracle would have taken a great power indeed.

She nodded slowly, turning in the direction of the island. "I have been having strange dreams. Recalling the faces of my parents. Places that in the past I may have been, but I do not recall them, and I do not know where they are."

She looked sad, wistful, almost. As if she wished that those dreams were real.

"Do you think the dreams are trying to tell you something?" I prompted; the Oracle had a habit of beginning to say something and then drifting off somewhere else—perhaps seeing things that were to come, or had been.

"There is one warning in the dreams. That I must *never* leave Nevertide. They, my parents, never say why… they just keep repeating the same warning, over and over again."

"Do you wish to return?" I asked.

She looked down, closing her eyes for a moment. The

shadows that flickered across her skin became darker and more insistent, their rapid movements suggesting her inner turmoil at such a question.

"I don't know!" she burst out suddenly. "I don't think I do. As much as my parents warn me of danger, another world calls to me—the world that contains the places in my dreams. Some are beautiful; magical lands that I wish to see, places I have never before witnessed in my visions of the future. I am tired of being so alone." She hesitated, her thin hand fluttering over her collarbone. "It is hard being someone who sees, but doesn't *see*. I witness all the great things that the worlds have to offer, and yet I can never take part in them myself... I hope that those who come after me won't suffer the same fate."

"Those who come after you?" I questioned.

She waved her hand dismissively.

"Not for a long time," she added.

I understood her plight. I knew what it was like to feel cut off from the world. If I hadn't met Sofia, I would be no different— still trying to chase what was human in me, what connected me to others, but getting nowhere. Forever lost in the dark.

"Your parents left you in Nevertide a long time ago," I said. "Perhaps they were afraid their families would try to destroy you. But it has been many, many years. The Ancients are no longer; the dangers may well have passed. If you do wish to explore the other dimensions—Earth, the In-Between or the rest of the supernatural world—know that you have a place of safety here."

She turned to me, her white-blue eyes flickering to mine for a brief moment before she started to look through me—that uncomfortable habit she had of making everyone feel like a ghost.

"Thank you, Derek of The Shade. I will remember that, and all your other kindnesses. I just wish I could see my own future… It is so dark and contorted. Since the moment I arrived here it has been unclear."

"Perhaps, when you settle on a decision, it may help."

She smiled softly, nodding.

"I think you are right. I will let you know what I plan. In the meantime"—she inhaled a gust of fresh air, her blonde hair whipping up behind her like freshly fallen snow—"I shall leave you in peace… There is much to come."

She vanished before I could ask her what she meant. I became irritated for a moment, before starting to laugh at myself.

Of *course* there was much to come. We were talking about GASP and the residents of The Shade. There was always some twist of fate or surprise waiting around the corner. I didn't need an Oracle to tell me that.

My musings were over. I wanted to go hunt down Sofia and kidnap her to the lighthouse for at least an hour, and then join the rest of our family for the evening.

Talking to the Oracle made me appreciate once again how

fortunate I was to be surrounded by those I loved—children, grandchildren, and I supposed soon great-grandchildren. These were the blessings of an extraordinary life, and if I had learned anything in my time on this immortal coil, it was that the strange twists and turns of our lives would always surprise me, always catch me unawares.

For that, I was grateful… As a member of the undead, it was what made me feel truly alive.

IS THIS THE END OF THE SHADE?
NO, IT ISN'T!
THERE WILL BE A SEASON 6!
WOO!

Dearest Shaddict,

Thank you for joining me on the epic journey that has been Season 5! This book, A Tide of War, concluded Season 5's story arc, however, I am excited to announce that I've decided to continue the Shade books for another season!

Book 42, **A Gift of Three**, will mark the beginning of Season 6, where you will return to The Shade and reunite with your favorite characters (and meet some awesome new ones) in a **brand new** pulse-pounding adventure!

Fresh romances, nail-biting suspense, and a mystery waiting to be unraveled…

Your Shade family awaits you in **A Gift of Three**, which releases **April 10th, 2017**. Not long to wait!

Pre-order your copy now and have it delivered automatically to your reading device on release day.

Visit: www.bellaforrest.net

Thank you for reading.

I will see you again very soon, back in The Shade…

Love,

Bella xxx

P.S. Join my VIP email list and I'll send you a personal reminder as soon as I have a new book out. Visit here to sign up: **www.forrestbooks.com** (Your email will be kept 100% private and you can unsubscribe at any time.)

P.P.S. Follow The Shade on Instagram and check out some of the beautiful graphics: @ashadeofvampire

You can also come say hi on Facebook:

www.facebook.com/AShadeOfVampire

And Twitter: @ashadeofvampire

CPSIA information can be obtained
at www.ICGtesting.com
Printed in the USA
FSOW01n0917251117
41641FS